# MARK TIDD IN THE BACKWOODS

# LECTOR HOUSE PUBLIC DOMAIN WORKS

This book is a result of an effort made by Lector House towards making a contribution to the preservation and repair of original classic literature. The original text is in the public domain in the United States of America, and possibly other countries depending upon their specific copyright laws.

In an attempt to preserve, improve and recreate the original content, certain conventional norms with regard to typographical mistakes, hyphenations, punctuations and/or other related subject matters, have been corrected upon our consideration. However, few such imperfections might not have been rectified as they were inherited and preserved from the original content to maintain the authenticity and construct, relevant to the work. We believe that this work holds historical, cultural and/or intellectual importance in the literary works community, therefore despite the oddities, we accounted the work for print as a part of our continuing effort towards preservation of literary work and our contribution towards the development of the society as a whole, driven by our beliefs.

We are grateful to our readers for putting their faith in us and accepting our imperfections with regard to preservation of the historical content. We shall strive hard to meet up to the expectations to improve further to provide an enriching reading experience.

Though, we conduct extensive research in ascertaining the status of copyright before redeveloping a version of the content, in rare cases, a classic work might be incorrectly marked as not-in-copyright. In such cases, if you are the copyright holder, then kindly contact us or write to us, and we shall get back to you with an immediate course of action.

**HAPPY READING!**

# MARK TIDD IN THE BACKWOODS

## CLARENCE BUDINGTON KELLAND

ISBN: 978-93-5336-096-2

First Published:                    -

LECTOR HOUSE LLP
E-MAIL: lectorpublishing@gmail.com

THEN I HEARD COLLINS SAY SOMETHING THAT SOUNDED LIKE
"WO-OO-OF!"

# MARK TIDD IN THE BACKWOODS

BY

## CLARENCE B. KELLAND

AUTHOR OF "MARK TIDD"

ILLUSTRATED

HARPER & BROTHERS PUBLISHERS
NEW YORK AND LONDON

# CONTENTS

# LIST OF ILLUSTRATIONS

# MARK TIDD IN THE BACKWOODS

## CHAPTER I

It all started just before school was out. One afternoon when I got home mother showed me a letter from Uncle Hieronymous, who lives in the woods back of Baldwin, on the Middle Branch of the Père Marquette River. I never had seen him, but he and mother wrote to each other quite often, and I guess she'd been telling him a good deal about me, that's Binney Jenks, and Mark Tidd and Tallow and Plunk. Of course, Mark Tidd was most important. He always thought us out of scrapes. So what did this letter of his do but invite us all to come up to his place and stay the whole summer if we wanted to?

As soon as I read it I was so excited I had to stand up and prance around the room. I couldn't sit still.

"Can we go, ma? Can we go?" I asked, over and over again, without giving her a chance to answer.

Ma had been thinking it over, because she said yes right off. Ma never says yes to things until she's had a chance to look at them from all sides and knows just what the chances are for my coming out alive. "You can go if the other boys can," she told me, and I didn't wait to hear another word, but went pelting off to Mark's house.

Mark was in the back yard talking to his father when I got there, and I burst right in on them.

"Can you go?" I hollered. "D'you think you can go?"

"L-l-light somewheres," says he. "You're floppin' around l-l-l-like Bill Durfee's one-legged ch-chicken."

"Can you go to my uncle Hieronymous's? We're asked in a letter. The whole kit and bilin' of us. Up in the woods. Right on a trout-stream. In a log cabin." I broke it all up into short sentences like that, I was so anxious. After a while Mark got it all out of me so he understood it, then he turned to his father.

"C-c-can I go, father?" he asked.

Mr. Tidd, though he'd got to be rich, was just as mild and sort of dazed-like and forgetful as ever—and helpless! You wouldn't believe how helpless he was.

"Way off into the woods?" says he. "Fishin' and sich like? Um-hum. 'S far's I'm concerned, Mark, there hain't a single objection, but, Mark, I calc'late you better see your ma. She sort of looks after the family more'n I do.... And if she lets you go, son, I'll give you a new set of Gibbon's *Decline and Fall* to take with you. You'll enjoy readin' it evenin's." With that he took out of his pocket a volume of old Gibbon and sat himself down on the back steps to read it. He was always reading that book and telling you things out of it. After I'd known him a year I most knew it by heart.

We went right up-stairs to where Mrs. Tidd was making her husband a shirt on the sewing-machine. She didn't *have* to make him shirts, because they had money enough from the invention to buy half a dozen to a time if they wanted to. But Mrs. Tidd, she says there ain't any use buying shirts for a dollar and a half when you can make them twice as good for fifty cents and a little work. That was her all over.

Mark called to her from the door. "Ma," he said, "can I go—"

She didn't let him get any further than that, but just says sharp-like over her shoulder: "There's a fresh berry-pie on the second shelf. Can't you see I'm so busy I dun'no' where to turn?"

"But, ma," he says again, "I d-d-d-don't want pie. I want to g-go—"

"No," says she, "you can't." Just like that, without finding out where he wanted to go or anything; but that didn't scare us a mite, for we knew her pretty well, I can tell you. In a second she turned around and wrinkled her forehead at us. "Where you want to go?" she rapped out.

Mark started in to tell her, but he stuttered so I had to do it myself. I explained all about it in a jiffy. She thought a minute.

"It'll get you out from underfoot," she says, "and keep us from being et out of house and home. I guess if the others can go you can."

You always could depend on Mrs. Tidd to be just that way. She was so busy with housekeeping or something, and had her head so full that she didn't get to understand what you said at first and always said no just to be safe, I guess. But I never knew her to refuse Mark anything that he had any business asking. For all her quickness we fellows thought a heap of her, I want to tell you.

When the Martins and Smalleys found out we could go they let Tallow and Plunk come along, so there we were. We fixed it to leave the day school was out and to stay just as long as we could hold out.

We started the day we planned. At first we thought we'd take a lunch, but Mrs. Tidd set her foot down.

"You'll need a hot meal," she told us, "so you go right into the dining-car when you get hungry." Then she gave Mark the money for our dinners, and we all kissed our folks good-by and got on the train.

It was pretty interesting riding along, and we enjoyed it fine till we got to Grand Rapids. We had to change there for Baldwin, and from then on the ride began to get tiresome. We tried a lot of things to pass away the time, but nothing helped. I guess it was because we were so anxious to get into the woods. We went along and along and along. I hadn't any idea Michigan was so big. After a while a colored man came in and yelled that dinner was ready in the dining-car. Mark began to grin. It looked like he was ready for the dinner. So was I, and the other fellows didn't hold back much. We went in and sat down at a little table. Each of us got a card that told what there was to eat. There were so many things it was hard to make up our minds, but finally we hit on the idea of every fellow taking something different, and so we got a look at more of it than we would any other way. We were about two-thirds through eating when all at once that car acted like it had gone crazy. I looked at the other three, and you never saw folks with such scared expressions in all your life. Their eyes bulged out, their mouths were open.

Well, sir, we just rose right up out of our chairs; that is, all of us did but Mark Tidd, and he was so wedged in he couldn't. It started with a crack that we could hear above the roaring of the train, then the car sagged down at the front end and began to bump and jump and wabble back and forth like a boat in a storm. We hadn't time to get scared—only startled. Then the car went over—smash! I don't believe anybody ever got such a jolt. The next thing I knew I was kicking around in a mess of rubbish with my head down and my feet up. Busted tables and dishes and chairs and folks were all scrambled on top of me. First off I thought sure it was the end of me, but I didn't hurt any place, and when my heart settled down below my Adam's apple I began squirming around to get loose.

I remember the first thing I thought about was its being so still. Nobody was hollering or groaning or anything. It surprised me and sort of frightened me. I squirmed harder and wriggled a table off me and pushed a chair away from the back of my neck. Then I sat up. You never saw such a sight. The car was lying on its side, and the lower side where I was was nothing but a jumble of things and people. And the whole jumble looked like it was squirming.

Next I thought about Mark Tidd. He was so fat and heavy I was afraid he'd be smashed all to pieces. I tried to call him, and at the third try I got out his name.

"Mark," says I, faint-like, "are you hurt?"

Over to the left of me, under a dining-table with its legs spraddled up, I heard a grunt—a disgusted grunt. It was a familiar grunt, a grunt that belonged to Mark.

"H-h-hurt," says he, sarcastic-like, but cool as a cucumber, only stuttering more than usual. "H-h-hurt! Me? Naw; I'm comfortable as a ulcerated t-t-tooth. Hey, you," says he to somebody down under the rubbish, "quit a-kickin' me in the s-s-stummick."

I knew he was all right then, and began figgering about Tallow Martin and Plunk Smalley. In a minnit both of them came sort of oozing out from amongst things looking like they'd sat down for a friendly chat with a cyclone.

"Mother'll be mad about these pants," says Plunk.

"There hain't much pants left for her to get mad about," says Tallow, angry-like and rubbing at his shoulder. "What you want to do is get a barrel."

"W-what *you* want to do," says Mark Tidd, "is g-git me out of here. There's a feller keeps k-k-kickin' me in the ribs and somebody t-t-tried to ram a table-leg into my e-e-ear."

Folks was digging their way out all around us now, and nobody seemed hurt particular, though some was making an awful fuss, specially a stout lady that had lost a breastpin. We began mining for Mark, and pretty soon we got down to where we could see him. He was the beat of anything I ever saw. Somehow he'd wriggled so as to get his head on a soft leather bag that somebody'd brought into the diner—most likely some woman. One arm was pinned down, but the other was free, and what do you think he was doing with it? Eating! Yes, sir; eating! He had two bananas in his pocket that he'd grabbed off the table just before the smash-up, and there he lay, gobbling away as calm as an iron hitching-post. It made me mad.

"You'd eat," says I, "if Gabriel was tooting his horn!"

"D-d-didn't know what was goin' to h-happen," says he, "so I th-thought I'd g-git what enjoyment there was t-t-to it."

We hauled him out, and it took all three of us. Heavy? I bet he weighs two hundred pounds. We got his head and shoulders free first and tried to drag the rest of him from under, but he wouldn't drag. Why, each one of his legs weighs as much as I do. He has to have all his clothes made special. I bet I could rip one of his pant-legs down the front, put sleeves in it, and wear it for an overcoat.

While we were tugging away at him somebody outside began smashin' the door, and pretty soon three or four men crawled in and began helping folks out. One of them came over to us and looked down at Mark.

"Hum," says he. "Didn't know there was a side-show aboard."

That made Mark kind of mad.

"Mister," says he, "this is the f-f-f-first wreck I was ever in, and I want to en-enjoy it. So I'd rather b-be pulled out by a f-f-feller that's more polite."

The man laughed. "Didn't mean to offend you," he said. "Beg your pardon. Naturally I'm one of the politest men in Michigan, but, you see, I was shaken up considerable by the wreck."

Mark grinned. "All right," says he. "Go ahead. I've got about all the f-fun there is out of bein' tangled up here."

The four of us hoisted him up and set him on his feet. He shook himself like you've seen a dog do when it comes out of the water, blinked around him to see what there was to see—and then took another banana out of his pocket and began to skin it absent-mindedly.

The man threw back his head and laughed fit to kill. "You sure *are* a cool one," he says.

"Don't do any good to g-g-get excited," says Mark. "There's always enough o-other folks to do that. Anybody hurt?"

"Haven't found anybody yet. It's a regular miracle."

Mark looked at Tallow and Plunk and me and shook his head. "You're the fellers that d-d-don't b'lieve in luck," says he. "Now I g-g-guess you won't make fun of my carryin' a horseshoe." And he pulled one out of his pocket. "Found this jest as we was gittin' on the train," he says to the man, "and l-look what it's done!"

"I'll never travel again without a horseshoe," he says. "Let's get out of here— we're the last ones."

"Got to git my hat," says Mark.

That was just like him. When he did a thing he did it thorough. If there'd been any danger and he ought to have got out he would have gone. He never took chances he didn't have to; but there wasn't any danger, so he wouldn't go until he took along everything that belonged to him. It took us twenty minutes to locate our stuff. The man helped us, laughing all the time. He seemed to think he was having a lot of fun. I sort of liked him, too. He was jolly and good-natured and pretty good-looking.

When we got outside I said to Mark, so the man couldn't hear, "Nice feller, ain't he?"

"Too g-good-natured," says he.

"You're mad 'cause he made fun of you."

"'Tain't that. He's one of these f-f-fellers that make a business of bein' p-pleasant. Maybe he's all right, b-but if I was goin' to have much to do with him I'd k-keep my eye on him."

"Huh!" says I; but after a while you'll see Mark wasn't so far wrong, after all. I never saw such a boy for seeing into folks. He could almost always guess what kind of a person anybody was.

We stood around a minute, getting our breath and sort of calming down. Then we watched the trainmen digging baggage and valuables out of the car and finding owners to fit them. That wasn't very interesting, so we went and sat down on the bank beside the track and commenced to wonder how long we would have to stay there.

"Probably have to wait for a train from Grand Rapids," Tallow said.

Mark got up and looked down the track. "G-g-guess they can crowd us in th-them."

Just then the good-natured man who helped us out of the wreck came along, grinning like he'd found a quarter on the sidewalk.

"Hello!" says he. "Any the worse for wear?"

"No," says Plunk.

"Camping?" says he.

"Sort of," says I. "Goin' to stay at my uncle's cabin."

"Whereabouts?" he asked.

"We git off at Baldwin," I told him.

"Good fishing?" he wanted to know.

"My uncle says it's bully."

He sat down alongside of us. "My name's Collins," says he—"John Collins."

He sort of waited, and then I introduced everybody, beginning with Mark Tidd, then Tallow Martin, who was next to him, then Plunk Smalley, and last of all Binney Jenks, which is me.

We talked considerable and speculated on how long we would have to wait and wished there was a lunch-counter handy—especially Mark. Maybe twenty minutes went along before we saw the conductor and yelled at him to know if we were going to have to stay all night.

"Better hustle up to the day coaches," says he. "I guess we can pull out pretty soon."

When we got in the car it was pretty crowded, but we four got seats together. Mr. Collins had to take half of a seat quite a ways off from us. I could tell by the way Mark's eyes looked that he was glad. For some reason or another he'd taken a dislike to the man. I couldn't see why, because he seemed to me to be pleasant enough for anybody.

I noticed that Mark had a piece of paper in his hand, crumpled up into a ball.

"What's that?" I asked him.

"D-dun'no'. Picked it up outside."

"Nothin' but a piece of paper, is it?"

"Looks so, but you n-n-never can tell." He opened it up, and it wasn't anything but a sheet of a letter. The writing began right in the middle of a sentence where the man who wrote it had finished one page and started another. I looked over Mark's shoulder and read it.

"—peculiar old codger," it said. "You'll have to be careful how you handle him. He'll smell a mouse if you don't step pretty softly, and then the fat will be in the fire. You haven't the description of the land, so here it is. Keep it safely, and bring back a deed. It will be the best day's work you ever did." Then came some letters and figures that we didn't understand, but we did understand them later. They looked mysterious and like a cipher code—"The S. 40 of the N. W. ¼ of Sec. 6, Town 1 north, R. 4 west." Then the letter was signed by a man named Williams J. Partlan.

"Wonder what it means?" I asked.

"Dun'no'," says Mark. "Guess I'll s-s-save it and find out."

Now, that was just like Mark. He didn't just wonder what these letters and figures meant and then throw away the paper; he saved it so he could study it out or ask somebody who could explain it to him. He was the greatest fellow for looking into things he couldn't understand you ever heard of.

It was hot and dusty, and pretty soon it began to get dark. First I knew Mark began slumping over against me until he almost squeezed me out of the seat, and then he began to snore. I poked him with my elbow, but it didn't do any good.

Once Mark Tidd gets to sleep it would take more than my elbow to wake him up. I bet he'd have slept right through the wreck and been picked out of it without ever missing a snore. After a while the conductor came through and called "Baldwin. Change for Manistee, Traverse City, and Petoskey." At that I had to wake Mark, so I put my mouth close to his ear and hollered. He lifted a big fat hand and tried to brush me away like I was a fly. I hollered again and poked him a good one in the ribs. He grunted this time, and with another poke and a holler he half opened his eyes and wiggled his head from one side to the other like he was displeased about something.

"We're coming to Baldwin," said I. "Wake up."

"I d-d-don't care," says he, stuttering like anything, "if we're c-c-comin' to Jericho with the walls a-tumblin' down."

But in a minnit he roused up, and as soon as he really got it through his head what was going on he was as wide awake as anybody.

After a little the train stopped at Baldwin, and we scrambled out, lugging our suit-cases. Out of the tail of my eye I saw Mr. Collins getting off, too. Well, sir, we got off at a little depot, smaller than the one at Wicksville. Down a little piece was a building with lights on it, and that was all. There wasn't any town that we could see, nothing but the two buildings.

"B-b-bet it's a lunch-counter," says Mark.

"Makes no difference if it is," says I. "We got to find my uncle, and you got to come along. If you don't we never will find him, for you're all he's got to go by. I never saw him, you know. When mother wrote we were coming she told him to look out for the fattest boy he ever saw, and that the rest of us would be along with you."

"Huh!" says Mark, disgusted-like.

We stood in front of the depot, looking around and waiting for uncle to come up and speak to us. Pretty soon we saw a man come along squinting at everybody and looking into corners and stretching his neck to see around people. He was a tall man, so tall his head come almost on a level with the top of the door. He had a mustache, too—the biggest one I ever saw, with ends that poked out past his cheeks and then swerved down until they almost touched his shoulders. He didn't have any hat on, and his overalls didn't come within six inches of reaching his shoes. I most laughed out loud.

When he came to us he stopped and looked and looked. It was mostly at Mark.

"Hum!" says he, after a minnit. "Fattest boy I ever see.... Fattest.... Boy." He reached out an arm as long as a fence-rail and pointed at Mark. "You're him," says he, and chuckled to himself. "Now, hain't you him?" He didn't wait for an answer, but said a little poetry. I found afterward he made it up on the spot.

> "I'm lookin' for a boy who is awful fat,
> But I didn't think you'd be as big as that."

Then he grinned the mostly friendly grin you ever saw.

"Hieronymous Alphabet Bell is my name," says he, "and I'm a uncle. Yes, sir. You wouldn't think to look at me I was an uncle, but I am. My nephew's name is Jenks. Does any one of you happen to be named Jenks?"

"I'm him, uncle," says I.

He stuck out his hand to me, and I shook with him.

"Howdy, nephew," says he. "Pleased to make your acquaintance." He was that polite! "What's his name?" he asked, pointing to Mark Tidd.

I told him, and they shook hands. After that he shook hands with Tallow and Plunk and acted like he was tickled to death to see us. When he'd done shaking hands once he commenced with me and did it all over again.

"Boys!" says he, making an exclamation of it. "I don't like boys. I jest despise boys. You can see I do, eh? Can't you, now? Tell it by my manner. They're nuisances, so they be, but I can tame 'em. No monkey-shines, mind, or look out for Uncle Hieronymous Alphabet Bell." After he said this he leaned up against the side of the depot and laughed and shook and slapped his hand against his thigh, but without making a sound. In a minnit he straightened up and recited another little poem:

> "Oh, boys is a pest,
> They give you no rest."

Mark was looking at Uncle Hieronymous with his eyes bunging out, as interested as could be. His little eyes, almost hidden by his fat, were twinkling away, and I could see right off that he liked uncle. That made me glad, for I liked uncle, too. There was something that made you sort of sorry for him. I guess it was because he was so glad to see us fellows. It made you think maybe he was pretty lonesome.

"Come on," says he. "I got an engagement with Marthy and Mary, so I got to hustle. Don't like to break no engagements."

"Girls?" I asked, feeling sort of offish about it.

"No," says he, "not exactly girls; nor yet exactly wimmin." And that was all he'd say about them.

We followed him over to a railing where he'd hitched his horse and wagon. As soon as he came within earshot of the horse he began talking to him just like anybody'd talk to folks.

"Good evenin', Alfred," says he; and I thought that was a funny name for a horse. "I'm back again," he says, "a-bringin' with me three medium-sized boys and one boy that is a little mite—say about a hundred pounds—over the medium." He turned to us. "Come over here," he says, "and see you act your politest. I want you should be acquainted with Alfred. Step right up. Alfred, this here is my nephew, Binney Jenks."

Alfred lifted his head and bobbed it down in as fine a bow as you ever saw, and he did the same thing when he was introduced to the other three.

"Be we glad to have visitors, Alfred?"

Alfred bobbed his head three times and whickered the most pleased whicker I ever heard a horse give.

Uncle turned to us solemn. "It's all right, fellers," says he. "I was a mite bothered till you'd met Alfred and I found out what he thought about you. If Alfred had took a dislike to you I don't know what I ever would have done. Alfred and Marthy and Mary sort of runs me, so to speak. The way they boss me around is surprisin' the first time you notice it."

We all climbed in the wagon with our baggage, and uncle leaned over the dash-board so Alfred could hear better.

"He's a leetle deef," uncle told us. Then he spoke to the horse. "Alfred," says he, "I calc'late we better be startin' if you feel you've got rested. I don't want to hurry you, but if you feel you're ready, why, jest go ahead."

Alfred turned his head as though he wanted to see everybody was in, then he sort of sighed and began to go up the road slow as molasses.

Pretty soon we came to the town, which was about a half a mile away from the depot and the hotel. We went through it without stopping, and then turned out into the country. In a few minutes we were right in the woods; not woods of great big trees, but woods of little trees. There wasn't anything but woods any place, and uncle said it was that way for miles and miles.

"Nothin' but jack-pine and scrub-oak," says he. "Timber's gone—butchered off. Once," says he, "you could walk through here for days and never git away from the pine."

We drove and drove and drove. In places it was so dark we couldn't see Alfred's tail, but he knew the way, and if it hadn't been for bumps and holes that jarred and joggled us we would all have been asleep before we got to uncle's house.

But we got there at last, and it was a log cabin. The front door was in the back, and there wasn't any back door in the front. What I mean is that there wasn't but one door, and that went into the kitchen.

"I figgered out," says uncle, "that the place folks wanted to git most often was the kitchen, especial after comin' off the river, so there's where I put the door." Then he recited another poem:

"This al' shack is sure a dandy;
Everything is neat and handy."

He led us through to the front of the house, where there was a bed and two cots for us. "Now," says he, "git to bed. Breakfast's at four, and Mary and Marthy'll be all wrought up to see you. Good night," says he, and off he went.

We were so tired we didn't stop to talk, but just tumbled into bed and were off to sleep in a minute. .

# CHAPTER II

Most likely we would have slept till noon that first morning at uncle's place, but he didn't let us. Uncle had an idea that day began as soon as you could see to get around without a lantern, and it didn't seem to me that I had finished slapping a mosquito that buzzed around me before I went to sleep when somebody jerked the cover off me and yelled, "Grub-pile." I got one eye open enough to see Uncle Hieronymous standing there grinning like all git out, and Mark and Tallow and Plunk squirming around disgusted in bed.

"Bacon's frizzlin'," says uncle. "I let you oversleep this mornin', figgerin' you was wore out. Come a-runnin'! Git up! Why, it'll be noon in a matter of eight hours!"

There was a smell of something coming in from the kitchen that waked me up quick. I got my feet out on the floor and looked over at Mark Tidd. He was sitting on the bed, with his pudgy nose pointing to the door and sniffing away with the happiest expression I ever saw on his face. Part of the smell was bacon, and part of it was frying potatoes, but the best of it was something else better than both of them put together, and I couldn't make out what it was.

"Hungry?" says Uncle Hieronymous.

Mark answered him. "I c-c-could eat the tail of the whale that s-s-swallered Jonah," says he.

We dressed in a hurry so we could get nearer to that smell. By the time we were washed uncle had everything on the table, and we rushed at it like we'd been fasting for forty days and forty nights. Then we saw where the best part of the smell came from. It was little fish all brown and crisp outside—a heaping platter of them.

"Troutses," says Uncle Hieronymous. "Leetle speckled troutses. Ketched by me personal right in my front yard, so to speak. Got 'em special for you jest before startin' to the station." Then he made up another little poem:

> "When you see a leetle trout
> You'd sooner eat than go without."

Nobody said another word until there wasn't a thing left on the table but little heaps of fish-bones. Uncle moved back his chair and grinned, and we all grinned back at him. We felt just like grinning. I don't know when I've felt so good.

"Marthy and Mary is waitin' to get acquainted with you," uncle says. "They're peculiar, Marthy and Mary is—most exceedin'ly peculiar—so you want to be p'tic'lar how you act. I wouldn't have Marthy and Mary get a bad idea of your mannerses for anythin'."

He shut the door tight and then went to the window.

"Marthy!" says he, as loud as he could yell. "Mary! Comp'ny to the house. Hey, Marthy! Hey, Mary!"

Well, sir, we didn't know what to expect, but in a minnit two pure-white cats came hustling out from among the underbrush with their tails sticking straight up in the air and the most interested expression on their faces you ever saw.

"Come here to the winder," says uncle to me. He put his head out and spoke to the cats. "Marthy and Mary," says he, "this here young person is my nephew, Binney Jenks. Git the name—Binney Jenks."

The cats both says "Miau," and reared up on their hind legs with their fore paws against the house.

Uncle Hieronymous sort of drew back. "Don't come a-jumpin' up here," he says. "I won't have it. You know better'n that, both of you. This here is Mark Tidd," he went on, "and this is Tallow Martin, and this is Plunk Smalley."

It didn't seem to me the cats was much interested in us, but uncle seemed to think they were all excited over our being there.

"Ree-markable cats," says he. "Intelligent! Oh, my, hain't they intelligent! Why, boys, the amount of brains them cats has got would s'prise the legislature down to Lansing."

He went to the stove and got some fish out of the frying-pan. "Marthy and Mary," he says, important and dignified-like, "I'm a-goin' to celebrate this here occasion by feedin' you troutses. Troutses hain't made for cats, except by way of markin' important happenin's. Chubs and perches is for cats, with maybe a bass or a pickerel, but troutses is for men almost exclusive. Here's one for you, Marthy, and here's one for you, Mary—and bear in mind, both of you, that you're much obleeged to these here boys. Lemme hear you say much obliged."

Martha and Mary both said "Miau," but I guess it was because they wanted the fish uncle was dangling over their noses.

"There," says he, drawing himself up as proud as a turkey-gobbler—"there. Intelligent, eh? Never saw cats like that before, *I* bet."

The cats sailed into that fish as enthusiastic as we boys had a little while before. Uncle gave each of them a couple. When they were through he spoke to them again.

"That's all," he says. "I hain't goin' to give you no more and be responsible for ruinin' your stummicks. Now go on off. D'you hear me? Go on off and catch mouses so's I can come out."

"C-c-can't you go out while they're there?" Mark wanted to know.

Uncle looked at him astonished. "What? Me? Go out with them two cats?" He shook his head two or three times and looked at Mark regretful-like. "I'm s'prised at you, Mark Tidd. O' course not. Never. Why," says he, "you can't never tell what cats'll do—especially white cats." He wagged his head again. I most laughed right there. Think of it! Uncle Hieronymous was afraid of his cats.

Marthy and Mary trotted off out of sight as obedient as could be, and uncle unlocked the door. It was our first look outside. Right in front of the house, which was made of logs, was a little stream. You could hear it gurgling and pouring along, and it sounded as pleasantly and neighborly as could be. All around was woods. The house sat in the middle of a clearing a couple of hundred feet wide, and beyond that all you could see was trees, trees, trees. The clearing was on a little rise of ground, and from the door you could look off across the brook for miles over what looked like a kind of swamp—not a squashy, boggy swamp, but a damp swamp where trees grew, and where, most likely, there was bears and maybe deer.

"Have you lived here always, uncle?" I asked him.

"Always? Me? Not always, not always, by any means. Fifteen years ago I lived up in what they call the copper country now. Yes, sir, right amongst it, so to speak, only I wasn't minin'. Not me. I owned a forty of timber and logged it a spell. Then along come a feller and offered me a price for it, and I up and sold to him. Yes, sir, sold out bag and baggage. No I didn't, neither." He commenced to laugh kind of as if there was a joke on somebody. "Friend of mine, he advised me I should keep the mineral rights, and, by gum! I own 'em to this very day. Me! Mineral rights. Haw!"

"What's m-m-mineral rights?" It was Mark asked him of course. None of the rest of us cared a whoop what mineral rights were, but Mark wasn't that way. You never could go mentioning anything strange around him without being made to put in a spell explaining it.

"Mineral rights," says Uncle Hieronymous, "is the rights to the minerals and metals and sich a-hidin' in the ground under a piece of prop'ty. One feller can own the trees, another can own the land, and another can own whatever happens to be found under the land. And that's what I own yet. Haw! If somebody was to up and find a di'mond-mine on that al' forty, who in the world would it b'long to? Why, to me, Hieronymous Alphabet Bell, and to nobody else that walks on two laigs."

Mark nodded that he understood, and then Uncle Hieronymous wanted to know what we figured on doing that day.

"L-l-let's explore," says Mark.

"We'll git lost," says I.

"Shucks. We won't go b-b-back into the woods. We'll just go along the b-b-brook."

"Good idee," says uncle. "Get acquainted with the neighborhood, so to speak. Whenever you git back'll be time to eat. If you get lost whistle like this," and he showed us a whistle that went, *"Wheet, wheet, wheet, whee, hoo."* "Reg'lar old lumber-camp signal," he says.

"D-don't you want to come?" Mark asked him.

"Me? Goodness, no! Couldn't spare the time. Couldn't spare a minnit. Got a lot of thinkin' to do to-day, and consid'able newspaper-readin', to say nothin' of washin' dishes and catchin' a mess of fish. No, I don't guess I got any time to spare. Why, there's things I've been plannin' to think about for weeks, and puttin' off and puttin' off. I picked to-day to study over 'em, and it's got to be done. I got to git out there and lay onto my back and figger out what I'd 'a' done if ever I'd got elected to Congress, and what keeps one of these here airyplanes up in the air; and another important p'int is why dogs wag their tails when they're tickled and cats when they're mad. You kin see I got my hands full.

"Some folks sit and think and think,
And some folks writes it down with ink,"

he finished up. "Them that thinks and writes it down," he says, "is authors and poets and philosophers, and them that jest thinks is loafers."

We were just getting ready to start out when a man that uncle called Billy came driving up in a rickety buggy. As soon as he got in sight he began to yell at us, but we couldn't understand what he was talking about. When he got close to the house he drew up and yelled louder than ever:

"Feller name of Collins here?"

"No," says uncle, scratching his chin. "We got a lot of names around, but Collins hain't one of 'em. Maybe some other'll do."

"It's a telegraft," says Billy, "and a dummed funny one, too. None of the boys around town could make head or tail to it. Collins was the name. Left word to the hotel he was goin' to stop somewheres on the Middle Branch. Mighty funny telegraft. Wisht I knowed what it was about."

"Maybe he's up to Larsen's," says uncle. "I've knowed folks to stop there that wouldn't hesitate a minnit to get telegrafts. Why, Billy, a feller there got a express parcel once."

Billy held a yellow envelope in his hand and shook his head at it. "Dummed peculiar!" he says. "The only words of sense to it is that somebody's comin' t' meet him. Want to see it?"

"Dun'no's I do, Billy," says Uncle Hieronymous. "I got most too much to figger about now without havin' more added unnecessary."

"Mysterious, I call it," Billy says, and shook up his horses. "You bet you I'm a-goin' to ask the feller what's the meanin' of it."

We watched Billy till he went out of sight around a bend in the sandy road; then Mark Tidd, with his little eyes twinkling the way they do when he sees something more than ordinary funny, says: "We b-b-better get started. There's consid'able j-jungle to explore."

Right off we knew Mark was going to pretend we were over in Africa or somewheres plugging along through a forest where the foot of white man had never trod or shot a gun or built a fire. [Note, by Mark Tidd: Must have been a trained foot.]

"I'll g-go first," says Mark. "Binney, you be the r-rear-guard. Plunk will watch to the right, and Tallow to the l-left."

So we started up-stream, keeping close to the water for fear of getting lost.

"Keep your eye p-peeled for boa-constrictors," says Mark. "Right here we don't need worry about n-n-natives, 'cause this part of the jungle is full of b-big snakes. Natives is terrified of snakes. If you begin to f-f-feel funny, lemme know. More'n likely it'll be a boa-constrictor t-tryin' to charm you. They kin do it. Yes, sir, they kin sit off a hundred feet and look at a man with them b-beady eyes of their'n and ch-ch-charm you so's you can't move."

It made us sort of shiver, because you never know what you're going to bump into in the woods, especially woods you don't know anything about. I never heard of any boa-constrictors in Michigan, but that wasn't any reason why some couldn't be there. There's lots in South America, and if one took a notion to crawl up to Baldwin I couldn't see anything to stop him. It would be quite a crawl for an ordinary snake, but a boa-constrictor, being so big, ought not to have much trouble about it.

"I'll be glad," says I, "when the Panama Canal is done."

"Why?" Mark asked.

"'Cause boa-constrictors won't be able to get acrost it," I says. "It'll be a purtection to the folks of the United States against the savage beasts that live in the Amazon jungles when they're to home."

Mark grinned. "I hain't n-never heard that exact reason given," says he, "for buildin' a canal, b-b-but I dun'no' but it's as good as a lot of others."

We went hiking along for another half an hour. All of a sudden Mark stopped and held up his finger. "S-s-s-savages," he whispered. In a jiffy we were all lying on our stummicks in the high grass, for, sure enough, we could hear a splashing in the stream that meant somebody or something was coming down toward us.

Almost without breathing we waited. Nearer and nearer the sound came, until a man showed up around the bend. He was wading right in the stream and flopping a fish-pole back and forth in the most ridiculous way you ever saw. He'd snap his line ahead till it touched the water and then snap it back and then snap it ahead again. Just like cracking a whip it was.

"Acts crazy," I says to Mark.

"Crazy nothin'," he says. "That's the way you c-c-cast a fly. He's trout-f-f-fishin'."

"Oh," says I, and watched him, more interested than ever. I'd heard about fly-casting, but somehow I hadn't expected to see anybody actually doing it. The man was maybe a hundred yards off, but we could see he had funny boots on that came way up under his shoulders. There was a little net hanging from his belt, and a basket with a cover over his shoulder. Pretty soon I heard Mark grunt surprised-like.

"What's matter?" I asked him.

"Know who he is?" Mark asked.

I looked close. The sun came through a place in the trees and shone right on his face, and I recognized the man. It wasn't anybody in the world but the Mr. Collins that helped us pull Mark out of the wreck.

"It was him the t-t-telegraft was for," Mark says to himself.

In five minutes Collins was almost in front of us. The water was to his waist, and he was wading slow. All of a sudden he stopped and pulled his pole up into the air. About thirty feet ahead of him something splashed in the water, and I could see his pole was bent way over.

"He's g-g-got one," Mark says, excited.

Sure enough, he had. It looked like a big one the way it pulled and jumped and sloshed around. Collins reeled and splashed around considerable himself, all the time getting closer to where we were. Then before you could say "Bingo" he stepped on something slippery—a smooth stone, I guess—and let out a yell. His feet went up and he went down *ker-splash*! For a second he floundered around like a hog in a puddle, throwing water all over the scenery, but he scrambled back onto his feet, with his pole still in his hand.

"He h-held it out of water all the t-t-time," says Mark, sort of admiringly. "He's the stick-to-it kind."

It's the way a fellow acts when he's alone that counts. Collins might have got mad and shook his fist and talked strong language, but he didn't. He just grinned kind of sheepish and went right on working with his fish till he got it close to him. Then he grabbed his little net and scooped it up.

"Whoop!" says he, taking it in his hand. "Ten inches, and speckled!"

Mark stood up. "D-do you always catch 'em that way?" he asked. "I never fished for trout, but if it's n-n-necessary to dive after 'em I calc'late I'll st-stick to perch."

Collins grinned first and then said: "Hello! What you doing here?"

"Explorin'," says Mark.

"Stopping near?"

Mark jerked his thumb back toward Uncle Hieronymous's.

"Who with?"

"His uncle," says Mark, pointing to me.

Collins looked more than ordinary interested. "Lemme see, you told me his name back on the train, didn't you? I don't remember it."

"D-d-don't b'lieve I did," says Mark.

"It's Hieronymous Alphabet Bell," says I, and Mark reached out with his foot and kicked me. The grass was so high Collins couldn't see him do it.

"Oh," says Collins, and he waded to shore. "Want to see my fish?"

We looked at it. It was a beauty, slender and graceful-like, with pretty red spots all down its sides.

Collins sat down and talked to us about fish and bears and deer and the woods, and then, the first we knew, he'd got the conversation around to Uncle Hieronymous. Mark looked at me and scowled, but I couldn't see why.

"He lives all alone, mostly," I told Collins, when he asked.

"I hear he's quite an interesting character," Collins said. "Guess I'll stop in and see him on my way down-stream. He won't chase me out, will he?"

I was just going to tell him uncle would be glad to see him when Mark spoke up:

"D-d-dun'no's I'd disturb him to-day," says he. "He's doin' somethin' special, and he's apt to take a dislike to anybody that in-interrupts him."

"Oh," says Collins. "I better put it off, then."

"Calc'late so," says Mark.

"Well, guess I'll start along. I'm going to be here a few days—up at Larsen's. Come to see me."

We said we would, and he started on down the stream.

As soon as he was out of sight Mark got up quick—quicker than I've seen him move in a dog's age—and ran down-stream maybe fifty feet, and then, right at the edge of the water, he stooped over and picked something up. From where I was I could see it was yellow. He sat right down and put it on his knee and began smoothing it out. We hurried over to see what he was up to.

"What you got?" Tallow asked.

Mark grinned and held up a yellow piece of paper.

"Telegraft," says he. "G-guess it's the one Billy b-b-brought."

"Collins drop it?" I wanted to know.

"I hain't seen n-nobody else go by," says Mark.

"What's it say?"

He'd got it all smoothed out now, and, though it was sopping wet and the ink had run quite a lot, he could read it. For a minnit he didn't say a word, but he had the most peculiar look on his face.

"Well?" says I.

He handed it over. At first I couldn't make head or tail of it. The last words were plain enough—"Coming by first train"—and the name that was signed was Billings, but the first part was Chinese to me. All the same, it kind of reminded me of something.

"Huh!" says I. "What's it about?"

Mark pulled another paper out of his pocket and handed it to me. It was the sheet of letter he picked up near the wreck.

"C-c-c-compare 'em," says he, with a peculiar grin.

I did, and the figures and letters were the identical same: "The S. 40 of the N. W. ¼ of Sec. 6, Town 1 north, R. 4 west." I was a mite startled, but, for all that, I couldn't see what there was to be startled about. I guess it was the way Mark acted.

"There's s-somethin' up," says he. "I bet a penny it's got somethin' to do with your uncle." He pinched his cheek and squinted his eyes like he always does when he's thinking, and then wagged his head.

"I don't l-like his looks. He's too dummed g-g-good-natured."

"But what's it all about?"

"How do I know?" he says, impatient. "I got to find out what these letters and figgers mean, hain't I? Then maybe I can sort of git an idee what he's thrashin' around for."

He got up and stuffed both pieces of paper into his pocket.

"Let's finish exploring and g-git back," says he. "I'm beginnin' to g-g-git hungry."

# CHAPTER III

When we got home Uncle Hieronymous was laying flat on his back by the side of the stream, with his eyes shut and the pleasantest smile on his face. He looked like everything he wanted in the world had walked right up and sat down in his lap. When he heard us coming he sat up and sort of wriggled his eyes to get them wide open, and made a funny motion at us with his hands. Then, right off, he made up a leetle poem:

> "Here they come with tired feet,
> Mosquiter-bites, and a wish to eat."

He got up slow, kind of one piece of him at a time, it looked, and then said:

"Hungry, eh? I bet you. What'll you eat? Will you have beefsteak, chicken-pie, strawberry short-cake, noodel soup, or bacon and eggs?" He reached around and scratched the back of his neck and winked one eye at the house. "If I was four boys with hollows into their stummicks I'd pick out bacon and eggs, I would. 'Cause why? 'Cause that's what they're goin' to get. Now, each one of you take your choice."

"N-n-name over those things again, please," Mark asked him.

Uncle did it as patient as could be. Mark thought careful, going over every one in his mind, then, as solemn as a screech-owl, he says, "I guess b-b-bacon and eggs look best to me."

Uncle nodded and looked at the rest of us. We spoke up for bacon and eggs right off without thinking over the other things, which seemed to satisfy Uncle Hieronymous all right.

"Will you have 'em baked, b'iled, fried, or stewed?"

"Fried, p-p-please," says Mark. "Once on the top and once on the b-bottom."

The rest of us took the same, and uncle went in to start a fire and begin his cooking. While he was at it we walked over to the little tumbledown barn off at a corner of the clearing. It looked as if something big and powerful had come along and given it a push, because it was all squee-geed. Boards were off, and what shingles were left stayed on the roof because they wanted to and not because they had to. Mark peeked inside.

"W-what's that?" he wanted to know.

The rest of us crowded around and then pushed inside. It was pretty dim in there, but as soon as our eyes got used to it we could see a long white thing laying across the beams above our heads.

"Looks like a boat," says I.

Tallow Martin lighted a match and held it up so we could see. Sure enough it *was* a boat—a canoe.

"W-wonder what it's doing here," says Mark.

"Let's ask Uncle Hieronymous," I says.

So we went off to the house, where uncle was standing over the stove, breaking an egg into a frying-pan.

"'Tain't ready yet," says he, as we came into the kitchen.

"We was just out in the barn," I says, "and we saw a canoe up on the beams. Does it belong to you?"

"Well, now, lemme see. Does that there curi'us leetle boat b'long to me or not? Now, *does* it? If you was guessin' how would you guess?"

"I'd guess it did," I says.

"Then," says he, "you'd be wrong, for it don't. At any rate, it didn't, last time I looked at it. But canoes is peculiar critters—no tellin' what it's up and done regardin' its ownership in nigh onto two months."

"Can we use it, uncle?"

"Use it? You don't mean git into the thing on the water? Into that there tipsy, oncertain, wabbly leetle boat? Would you dast?"

"S-s-sure," says Mark. "I learned to paddle one two years ago."

"Then," says uncle, "I guess nobody'll objec' serious to fussin' around in it. Feller left it here two years ago and hain't never called for it. Go ahead, boys, and do your worst."

The egg had been sizzling away in the frying-pan. Uncle poked at it with a fork, and then, quicker than a wink, he took hold of the handle of the pan, gave it a little flip, and, would you believe it, that egg turned over just as neat and settled down on its face. I heard Mark chuckle. Uncle looked sort of surprised.

"D-d-do you always turn them like that?" Mark asked.

"How would a feller turn an egg?" uncle wanted to know.

"Well," says Mark, "after seeing it done like that I don't know's there's any way quite so g-g-good. Anyhow, n-n-none so interestin'."

In about five minutes the eggs, with fried potatoes and bacon and coffee, were ready, and we put them where they were wanting to go. Uncle gathered up what was left, and when he had shut the door tight he called Martha and Mary and gave it to them.

"Can we get the canoe down now?" I asked uncle.

"You can git it down any time you want to exceptin' yestiddy. I don't allow nobody to do anything yestiddy around this house. No, sir. Not a single, solitary thing. That's how set in my ways I am."

We all went out to the barn, uncle bringing a ladder with him. He set it up against a beam, and in no time the canoe was down on the ground.

"Kind of a slimpsy-lookin' thing," he says, disgusted-like.

"Where's the p-p-p-paddles?" Mark wanted to know.

"Under the bed," says uncle, and I ran to get them.

We hauled the canoe down and put it in the water, but right away it began to leak, so we dragged it out again and asked uncle for some paint. He said green paint was all he had. Mark allowed that green paint wasn't exactly suitable for a canoe, but any paint was better than no paint, so uncle got a can and a brush off a shelf in the kitchen and brought them out to us.

We put the canoe up on a couple of logs and started in to paint, but after we had been at it a couple of minutes Uncle Hieronymous shook his head and grunted. Then he recited another poem:

> "Don't think that that's the way to paint,
> Because, my friends, it surely hain't."

Then he took the brush away from Tallow, who had it at that particular minute, and told us to clear out while he did a job of painting that would be a credit to the state of Michigan, even if the Governor were to come along to see it, with all the legislature marching in circles around his hat-brim.

We decided to explore down-stream this time. Just as we were starting out from the house Billy came driving along with a fat man on the seat beside him. Not just a big man, but a man that was as fat as Mark Tidd. Billy called to us and waved his hand, and we waved back. Then we started out.

"C-c-couldn't mistake that feller on a d-d-dark night," says Mark.

"It ain't apt to matter whether we do or not," I told him.

"N-n-n-never can tell. He's the man that's comin' to help out Collins. Wish I knew what those letters and figures in that telegram were about."

"Oh, come on, and forget about that. Let's find out what kind of country is down that way."

To go down-stream we had to take a path through heavy underbrush. Most of the time we had to force our way because the bushes were trying to cover the path. It wasn't very light, and it was boggy. About a hundred yards ahead we came to a little brook that emptied into the Middle Branch, with two saplings across it for a bridge. I was going ahead. No sooner had I stepped my foot off the far end of the bridge than something began to thrash around and rustle the reeds right under my feet, and all of a sudden a little animal about as big as a dog, or maybe a cat, jumped up and whisked out of sight. He scared me almost out of my wits.

"What was that?" says I.

"That," says Mark, "was a f-f-full-grown g-grizzly bear."

"G'wan!" says I. "There ain't no bears around here."

"Maybe not," says Mark, in a whisper, "but there's something else." He pointed, and there, across the stream, not more than a couple of hundred feet off, were two little deer and a big one.

Well, it startled all of us. Somehow until then we didn't realize we really were in the woods—the real, genuine, wild woods where big animals might be. I thought over what I'd said about bears and sort of changed my mind.

"You can't tell," I whispered back; "maybe there *is* bears."

The deer smelled us, I guess, and off they went, running with the funniest, jumpiest gait you ever saw.

"Did you notice," asked Mark, "that he asked w-w-who we were?"

"Who asked?" Tallow wanted to know.

"The f-fat man in Billy's wagon. I could see him asking Billy."

"Huh!" says I, and on we went.

After a while the ground got higher, and about two miles down we came to a place where the banks of the stream were maybe forty or fifty feet high. Then the stream widened out into a big pool and curved off to the right. It was a dandy place. We sat down, with our feet hanging over, and looked at the water. I noticed some black spots that moved around here and there toward the lower end of the pool where there wasn't any current, and after a while I got it through my head they were fish—trout. Great big fellows they were. I showed them to the other three, and we sat looking at them, watching how they stayed right around that spot, having a sort of fish meeting, I guess.

The sun was shining bright right down on the water, so that we could see to the bottom where the current didn't make a ripple. It was pretty deep in spots, too, where the water rushing down had scooped out a hole. It swept around that corner faster than anywhere above.

"Here comes somebody," says Tallow, and, sure enough, down-stream waded a man, casting away just like we had seen Collins do in the morning. He was an old man—we could tell by the way he carried his shoulders—and he looked tall. He came along, paying no attention to anything but his casting, wading right in the middle of the stream. We watched him without saying anything until he was almost under us.

"If he don't look out he's going to wade right into that hole," says Plunk Martin, but nobody thought to do anything except Mark, and he yelled down:

"L-l-look out, mister. You're goin' to s-s-step into a hole."

The man stopped, looked up, took another step, and sort of stumbled. Then he recovered his balance and waded to shore, but his landing-net had got loose from his belt and was floating down without his noticing it.

"You've lost your net," Tallow yelled.

The old gentleman started after it, but the water got deeper and the current dragged at him pretty strong. He was going to keep on, though, until Mark called to him again.

"It'll lodge right there in the b-b-brush-heap," he says.

We all scrambled down the bank to where the old gentleman was. He smiled at us pleasant-like, and said: "Much obliged, boys. I'd have got a good ducking if it hadn't been for you, and a ducking is no joke at my age."

"There," says Mark, "your net's c-c-caught. Go get it, Binney."

I scrambled around the shore to the brush-pile and crawled out to where the net was. It was easy to get.

"Camping around here?" asked the old gentleman. I guess he was close to seventy, because his hair and mustache were white as could be. He was a nice-looking old gentleman, with blue eyes that looked like they were twinkling at you, and a big nose. Not a homely nose, but a big one that looked as though he amounted to something.

"We're staying with my uncle Hieronymous," I told him.

He sat down on the bank to talk with us. It turned out his name was Macmillan and that he was a lawyer in Ludington, which is about forty or fifty miles farther, and on the shore of Lake Michigan. Right off when he said he was a lawyer Mark was interested. I could see it by the way he squinted his little eyes and pulled on his fat cheek.

"M-m-mister Macmillan," says Mark, "I want to show you s-somethin'."

"All right, my son, go ahead."

"I want to f-f-find out what it is, because it may b-be important."

"Let's have a look, then."

Mark took a paper out of his pocket and gave it to Mr. Macmillan. "I've been wonderin' w-w-what kind of a cipher that is," says he, "or w-w-what it is if it isn't a cipher. It m-m-means somethin'."

"'The S. 40 of the N. W. ¼ of Sec. 6, Town 1 north, R. 4 west.' Hum. Does look mysterious, doesn't it. But, my son, like a lot of things that look mysterious, it isn't so a bit when you know about it. That is nothing but the description of land. You know there has to be some way of describing every farm, no matter what its size or shape may be, so that everybody will know just where to find it. Well, this cipher, as you call it, describes a farm of forty acres that is the northwest part of Section Six of township number one west of range seventeen. That's all. Did you think it was telling where hidden treasure was hidden?"

Mark shook his head. "Maybe 'tis," says he, and all the afternoon we couldn't get another word out of him.

The rest of us talked with Mr. Macmillan and listened to stories about where he'd fished and hunted, and all about how this part of the state used to be a great pine forest that was butchered off and floated down-stream to the mills. I tell you it was interesting. It began to get late before he was half through, and he had to start for the place where his team was hitched.

"If you come to Ludington," says he, "drop in to see me."

We said we surely would.

"And you, young man," says he to Mark, "when you have any more mysteries to clear up just let me know."

Mark nodded as sober as could be. Anybody would think he expected to have a couple of mysteries every day.

Mr. Macmillan went off, and we turned back home. As soon as we got in sight of the house we saw uncle had company.

# CHAPTER IV

Two men were sitting on the steps, and uncle, tilted back in a chair, was facing them. Nobody seemed to be saying anything as we came up. When we were right close uncle turned and grinned at us.

"Comp'ny, boys," says he. Then he poked his finger at one visitor. "Jerry Yack," he says, and Jerry jerked his head. Uncle prodded at the other man. "Ole Skoog," he says, and Ole jerked his head just like Jerry did. Uncle clean forgot to mention our names at all. It was pretty much of a one-sided introduction, I thought.

We sat down, and nobody said a word. I could see Mark Tidd studying Ole and Jerry and sort of shaking his head over them like he couldn't make them out. They did nothing but sit and look straight in front of them. They looked like twin brothers, both big and bulging with muscle, both with china-blue eyes and pale hair and cheeks that showed pink through the sunburn.

"Are they brothers?" I whispered to uncle.

"Brothers? Who? Them fellers? Naw. They're Swedes. That's what makes 'em look alike. All Swedes look alike. Didn't you know that? Why, Binney, over in Sweden, where they come from, each feller wears a tag with his name on it. Only way to tell 'em apart. Heard once of a feller losin' his tag and wanderin' around for days without bein' able to find out who he was. When he did find out he found out wrong and had to be somebody else besides himself all the rest of his life. It's worryin' about that happenin' that makes all Swedes so melancholy."

"Oh!" says I. Mark's little eyes were opened up wide, and he was staring at uncle like all git-out. Couldn't quite make up his mind if uncle was fooling us or not.

About fifteen minutes later Jerry Yack hunched his shoulders and moved around uneasy-like. He opened his mouth once and shut it again. Opened it and shut it another time. Then he coughed. Seemed it took all that work to get ready to say something.

"Ay tank," says he, "ay bane goin'."

Ole looked up and did considerable wriggling himself. After a while he got ready to speak: "Ay tank," he says, "ay bane goin', too."

They both looked at uncle with their blue eyes wide open like babies. Uncle didn't say anything. After quite a spell Jerry got around to speak again. He asked a question of uncle.

"W'at you tank? Eh? You bane goin' —yess, or you bane goin' —no?"

Uncle shook his head and recited a poem that made Ole and Jerry look puzzled as anything:

"Shall I go or shall I stay?
That I must decide to-day."

He waggled his head at us boys. "That hain't neither exactly nor precisely the fact," says he; "it's you boys got to decide. Ole and Jerry here come to git me to help 'em a week or so on the river. Loggin'. Jerkin' logs out of the river-bed. River-bed's covered with timber farther down. It's timber that sunk in the old lumberin'-days, and there's a heap of it. They got a scow with a derrick onto it. What think?"

"H-h-how do you git the logs out?" Mark wanted to know.

Right off his curiosity got to working.

"Poke around with a pike-pole till you find a log. Git a chain fast around her, start your engin' goin', and jerk her out with the derrick. Pile 'em on shore."

Mark nodded like he understood. "How came the logs to be in the river?" he asked.

"Got water-logged and sunk when rafts was runnin' down," says Uncle Hieronymous. "Now, you four git together and decide if I can go. I'll be gone maybe two weeks. Dun'no' jest where I'll be, but somewheres on the river below. Plenty of grub in the house, plenty of fish in the stream. Nothin' to hurt you. How about it, eh?"

"Go, far's I'm concerned," I told him.

"M-m-me too," says Mark; and the rest joined in.

"Won't be afraid?" asked Uncle Hieronymous. "Sure? Don't mind bein' alone with Marthy and Mary, eh? Now be sure. Don't forgit them two white cats when you're thinkin' it over."

"We hain't f-f-forgot 'em," says Mark. Then he up and asked another question. "What I'm wonderin'," he says, "is, did Mr. Skoog and Mr. Yack ask you all that themselves or did they bring it written in a l-l-l-letter?"

"They—fetched—a—letter," he wheezed.

Mark nodded. "I d-d-didn't b'lieve they could have s-s-said it all," he says.

"When you going?" I asked.

"Right after we eat," says uncle, and with that he got up and commenced getting supper. In half an hour all seven of us were crowded around the little table, and I want to say if Ole and Jerry couldn't talk they could eat. If all Swedes eat like they did I bet the farmers in Sweden have to raise whopping big crops to have enough to go around.

After supper Jerry and Ole got a buckboard out of the barn and hitched their horse to it. Uncle threw in a canvas bag of clothes and climbed in.

"If you git to needin' anything you kin git it up to Larsen's, I guess," uncle said. He was going to say something else, but right in the middle of it the old horse jumped all his feet off the ground and started down the road a-kiting. Uncle and Ole and Jerry came pretty nearly being left behind. They all keeled over in a heap, with arms and legs waggling in the air, and there wasn't any good reason why all of them weren't jounced out on the ground in the first fifty feet. But they weren't. Finally Ole got to his feet and caught hold of the lines. He pulled and sawed and yelled, but on the old horse went until he jumped out of sight around a bend in the road. I heard Mark Tidd chuckle.

RIGHT IN THE MIDDLE OF IT THE OLD HORSE JUMPED ALL HIS FEET OFF THE GROUND AND STARTED DOWN THE ROAD A-KIT-ING

"B-b-bet those Swedes never started anywhere as quick as that b-b-before," he says.

I looked at him sharp. He had his sling-shot in his hand.

"Did you shoot the horse?" I asked, sort of provoked, because it didn't look like a polite thing to do.

He nodded yes.

"What for?" I asked.

He pointed up the road toward Larsen's, and there, coming along as fast as they could walk, were Collins and the fat man we saw in Billy's wagon that afternoon. "Th-th-that's why," says Mark.

"What have they got to do with it?"

"I got a sort of f-f-feelin' I don't want those f-f-fellows to see your uncle Hieronymous. Dun'no' jest why, but that's the way I f-f-feel."

"Well," says I, "they won't see him for a couple of weeks now."

"Not if you f-f-fellers don't blab where he is," says Mark.

"You needn't worry," I says, sharp-like. "Guess we can keep our mouths shut if there's any need."

"May be no need," says he, "but k-k-keep 'em shut, anyhow."

We watched the fat man and Mr. Collins. They were headed for our house, all right. I don't know why, but right there I began to feel that maybe Mark Tidd had stumbled onto something that wasn't just exactly the way it ought to be. It was hard to believe it, though, for Mr. Collins was such a pleasant, jolly sort of a man, and the fat man looked so good-natured he wouldn't brush a fly off his bald spot for fear of hurting its feelings. But things did look peculiar. That letter and telegram and the way Mr. Collins seemed to want to meet Uncle Hieronymous made it look as if they were in the woods for something more than a fishing-trip.

Mr. Collins called to us when he was quite a ways off. "Hello, fellows!" says he. "Had any luck to-day?"

We shook our heads. In a minnit they were in the clearing and in another were standing right by us.

"My friend, Mr. Jiggins, boys," says Mr. Collins, and then he went over all our names careful. "He's come up to fish, but I don't believe there's room enough for him in the stream. Do you?"

"Well," says Mark, "him and me would f-f-fill it perty full."

It was the first time I ever heard Mark Tidd joke about his own fatness, and it surprised me considerable. But he had a reason, most likely. He usually had a reason for what he did.

"Been having visitors?" asked Mr. Collins.

"Visitors?" says Mark, and looked as dull as a sheep. You wouldn't have thought, to look at him then, that he knew enough to spell fish without putting a "g" in it.

"Oh, I just saw somebody drive away."

"Yes," says Mark. "Went p-p-perty fast, too."

"Did seem to be in a hurry," says Mr. Jiggins.

Mark winked at me, and it was a minnit before I understood what he wanted. Then I knew it must be something about uncle, and there was only one thing about him right then, which was that he was gone away. I guessed Mark wanted me to tell it.

"It was my uncle Hieronymous," I says, and Mark nodded his head, satisfied.

"Going to town?" asked Mr. Jiggins.

"Dun'no'," says Mark. "He d-d-didn't say."

"Be gone long?"

"Won't be b-b-back to-night," Mark stuttered.

Mr. Collins looked at Mr. Jiggins, and Mr. Jiggins looked at Mr. Collins.

"We thought we'd drop in and call on him," says Collins.

"Too bad he's gone," I says. "Come again."

"We'll do that," says Jiggins; but he looked pretty disappointed, and I noticed him eying the road back to Larsen's. So did Mark. His little eyes twinkled kind of mean.

"Quite a walk d-d-down here, ain't it?" he asked, with his face solemn. "Dun'no's I'd care to walk it for n-n-nothin'."

"Dun'no's I would, either," said the fat man, pretty short. "Let's start back," he says to Collins.

"When uncle gets back I'll tell him you were here," I promised, and they said thank you.

"L-l-let's git something to eat," says Mark, and the way he stuttered to get it out was a caution. I've noticed he stutters worse when he's hungry than when he isn't. "I'll cook," says he, "if you fellers will wash the dishes."

There's no denying Mark was a good cook. He ought to be, for there never was anybody who thought more about eating than he did. He was always hanging around the kitchen watching his mother, and I'll bet there never was a girl who could make better baking-powder biscuits than he did that night. There were some raspberries Uncle Hieronymous had found time to pick, and lots of ordinary stuff like fried potatoes and ham.

"T-t-to-morrow," says Mark, "I'll make a pie." He stood looking out of the window, thinking a minute. Then he turned sudden-like, and frowned so his forehead got all ridgy. "Careless," says he. "Here we are, surrounded by hostiles, and the c-c-c-canoe right there under their eyes. N-n-never would be there in the mornin'. Hain't you f-f-f-fellers read any books? Don't you know folks fixed like we are always hide their canoe? Well, you b-b-better git right at it."

"It's all paint," says Plunk Smalley.

"P-p-p-paint!" Mark says, disgusted as could be. "What's p-paint against losin' our boat? Where'd we be if we lost it, I'd like to know? Hundreds of m-m-miles from civilization. Our only hope of gittin' back alive is that b-boat."

Off we went in a hurry, I can tell you. It seemed real. That was a way Mark had: he could make the games you played with him seem like you were doing the things in earnest. We took that canoe, paint and all, and hid it down the path that ran through the underbrush. We piled limbs of bushes all around it, hid the paddles near, and then went back to the house.

"That was a narrow escape," Mark says. "Wish we had it provisioned, but it don't look possible. We can p-p-put blankets and things in it, anyhow."

We did. We put blankets and matches and cooking-things near the canoe just as if we expected we might have to run to it for our lives any second. That didn't satisfy Mark. He made us fix up a pack full of canned things and potatoes and flour and salt so we could grab it and be off without waiting even to think. And all the time we thought it was just a game. We thought he was playing, while Mark never said a word, but just let us go on thinking so. *He* wasn't playing, though. He was looking ahead and getting ready if an emergency came up. Afterward he told me he wasn't sure we would ever need the boat, but there was just a chance, and if that chance happened we'd need it bad and quick. So he got it ready. That's why folks always have found it so hard to beat Mark Tidd. He'd sit and figure and figure and guess what might happen, and when he'd guessed every possible thing that could manage to come about he'd get ready for every one of them.

By the time the canoe was all ready it was almost dark. It was the first we'd thought about spending the night all alone in the cabin, way off miles from anybody, and I'll admit I began to feel pretty funny. I noticed everybody else was getting quiet and not saying much and looking every once in a while into the woods. It was chilly and still.

"L-l-let's go to bed," Mark says, after a while.

"Shall—shall we have a guard?" Tallow says, hesitating-like.

"No need," Mark says.

I began to think I would like to have somebody big—somebody big and so strong that knew so much about the woods. If some one like that had been there to sleep alongside of us not one of us would have worried a mite. But he wasn't, so we had to do without.

We put out the lights and locked the door, and after quite a while we all went to sleep.

# CHAPTER V

The next day we didn't do much but fuss around. Plunk and Tallow tried fishing for trout with angleworms, but they got only one, and he was a rainbow. Mark found a shady spot and read all the time he wasn't cooking or eating, and I got out Uncle Hieronymous's draw-shave and found a piece of seasoned hickory he had stowed away. First off I didn't know what I'd make of it, but after I'd figured a spell I decided it would be a bow and arrow. I was pretty handy with tools, and this wasn't the first bow I ever made, by any means. It took me all day to finish it and half a dozen arrows, so my time was filled up all right.

"Tell you what let's do," says I, at the supper-table. "Uncle said there was a lake about a mile off with bass and perch in it. What's the matter with digging some worms and hiking there early in the morning? Maybe we can catch a mess for dinner."

"G-g-good idea," says Mark. "Then let's get there by daylight."

We took a spade and went out back of the barn to dig worms. The ground was pretty dry, but by digging over about an acre we got a half a canful.

"Think it's enough?" I asked.

"All you can g-g-get has got to be enough," says Mark, which was perfectly true. Anyhow, if we got one fish for every worm we would have more than we could eat.

Uncle had an old alarm-clock that would still run considerable. I wouldn't go so far as to say it would run just right, but it had two hands and a face, and it ticked. That ought to be enough for any clock. And it did alarm. I should say it did! It went off like the crack of doom.

"What time'll I set her for?" I asked.

"'Bout two o'clock," says Tallow.

Mark grunted. "Two n-n-nothin'," he stuttered. "Three's plenty early."

Then we went to bed. We didn't seem to be as nervous that night as we had been the night before, which was pleasant. I don't like to be scared. It is one of the most disagreeable things that happen to me. I was just dozing off when Mark spoke to me.

"Those f-f-fellers was here to-day," he says.

"What fellers?" I asked, cross-like, because I didn't like being roused up.

"C-C-Christopher Columbus and George W-W-W-Washington," he says, disgusted. "Who'd you think?"

"You mean Collins and the fat man?"

He grunted: "Uh-hup. While you was back of the barn whittlin'," he says. "They went off disappointed. Seems like that f-f-fat feller don't care much for walking."

"What did you tell them?"

"Told 'em your uncle wouldn't be b-b-back 'fore night."

"Oh, go on to sleep," Tallow snorted, from his bed; and so Mark and I kept quiet, and the first thing I knew I was being waked up by the worst racket I ever heard. It scared me so I jumped out of bed way into the middle of the room. For a minnit I couldn't make out what was going on. It might have been a bear tearing down the house or an attack by Indians, for all I could make out. Then I got really waked up and recognized it was the old alarm-clock. It didn't seem like I'd been to sleep at all, and it was so dark a black cat would have looked sort of gray if it had come into the room. The other fellows were stirring around.

"Time to get up," I says.

"Doggone that clock," says Tallow.

I guess that's what we all thought, but nobody was willing to be the first one to back out, so we lighted a lamp and dressed. My, but it was chilly! When we opened the door and started outside it was like to frost-bite our ears. And everything was wet with dew; my feet were soaked before I'd gone a hundred feet.

I don't know what time it really was. Maybe it was three o'clock, but if it was, three is a heap earlier than I ever imagined it could be. Why, it was as dark as midnight. We stumbled around and found the road. It was about a mile up the road to the bridge, and maybe a half a mile across the stream to the lake. We came near missing it altogether in the dark, and we would have if it hadn't been for the sound of a frog splashing into the water. We turned off and fumbled down to the shore, and there we were. We might as well have been home, for we never could find the boat uncle told me about in that blackness, so we just sat down and grumbled. It was pretty uncomfortable, I want to tell you. All the fun there is crouching down in the dark on the shore of a lake you can hardly see, with your feet wet and shivers chasing each other up and down your back, can be put in your ear.

"Who thought of this?" Tallow growled.

"Binney," says Plunk.

"Who wanted to get up at two?" I asked right back, and they didn't have another word to say.

We huddled around, all fixed to quarrel. It got a little lighter, but not enough to do any good, and by that time we were hungry. Tallow mentioned *he* was, and Mark—the only one in the crowd to think ahead—pulled a bag out of his pocket with sandwiches and store-cookies in it. We gobbled them and felt a bit better.

Just as it began to get sort of grayish we heard wagon-wheels in the road.

Right off Mark started a game. He figured we'd feel better if we had something to think about, I guess.

"Hist!" says he. "The p-p-pirates!"

We all kept so still you couldn't even hear us breathe.

"If they f-f-find us here in their lair," says Mark, "it'll be all day with us. Have you got the diamonds s-s-safe, Binney?" he whispered.

"Yes," says I, feeling of some pebbles in my pocket, "I got 'em."

"Maybe they'll pass without seein' us," Tallow guessed.

But the wagon stopped. It stopped right alongside of where we were, and somebody spoke.

"Fine time of the day to get a man out," he says. "Might have had four hours' sleep yet."

"Never mind," says another voice, sort of laughing; "you'll be all right as soon as they start biting.... That boat Larsen told us about ought to be right near here."

"Let it stay," grumbled the other man. "I ain't going to stir out of this wagon till it's light enough for me to see to get around without busting my neck. A man of my size ain't a cat, to run along on the top of a fence."

"Here, have a smoke. That'll cheer you up. It'll be plenty light in fifteen minutes, Jiggins."

Mark nudged me. I thought the voices were familiar, but as soon as that name Jiggins was mentioned I knew it was Mr. Collins and the fat man.

"Lay low," says Mark, "and listen. That's the pirate chief."

We listened.

"We want to get back to Larsen's by nine o'clock," said Jiggins. "Our friend with the name ought to be home by this time, and I don't want to hang around this forsaken hole in the woods all summer."

"Hieronymous Alphabet Bell," says Collins. "That is quite some name. Wonder where he got it?"

"Don't care where he got it. What I'm worrying about is, will we get him?"

"Sure," says Collins. "He's probably forgotten he ever owned forty acres in the Northern Peninsula, and if he remembers it he won't think about retaining the mineral rights when he sold it."

"You never can tell about these old codgers. Some of 'em are wiser than they look."

"Well," says Collins, "we've *got* to land him. It means considerable to you and me, eh? To think of the old codger living here in the backwoods when he is the owner of one of the finest bits of copper property in the state! I don't suppose there's any telling what that land is worth as it stands."

"You can bet it's worth considerable, or the company wouldn't be so anxious to get hold of it. Anyhow, it would be enough to make our friend Hieronymous richer than he ever dreamed of being."

"Well, he won't ever know it. Seems kind of mean, sometimes, to gouge an old fellow, but I suppose business is business. He's as happy without it, likely."

"We haven't got it yet," snapped Jiggins, "and you want to move pretty cautious. Remember, you're a friend of a farmer who bought that piece to farm on. Remember he's a peculiar old fellow who wants to feel nobody else has any right whatever in the land he lives. That's why he wants to get the mineral rights Mr. Hieronymous Alphabet owns. Remember that. It ought to fool him, all right, but you can't ever tell. We mustn't offer him too much, or he'll get to thinking. Two hundred is the highest, I should say."

"Two hundred's plenty. There's no need to waste money, anyhow."

Mark Tidd was holding onto my arm. As Collins and Jiggins went on talking I could feel him getting more and more excited by the way his fingers dug into me. I hadn't any idea he was so strong in the hands, but I began to think he'd take a chunk right out of me.

"Quit it," I says, in a whisper.

"D-d-did you hear?" he asked, stuttering so he could hardly get the words out.

"Yes," says I.

Just then Plunk Smalley, who always was doing something at the wrong minnit, had to lean forward suddenly and bang his head against a stump.

"Ouch!" he hollered.

The talk in the wagon stopped in a second, and I heard somebody leap to the ground and come jumping toward us. Of course, it was Collins, because the fat man never could have moved so fast. We were in a nice place—all sitting on the ground, without the slightest idea where to run without getting mired or tangled up in the underbrush. But we did our best. Everybody took a different direction, and you could hear folks floundering wherever you listened. The fat man had got down and was coming after us too.

"Who was it?" he yelled to Collins.

"I don't know," Collins yelled back, "but I'm going to get them, anyhow." His voice sounded like he meant it, too.

Mark and Tallow and Plunk and I began getting together again, and, all in a crowd, we plunged ahead without looking where we were going. It was starting to get light now—light enough so you could see things dim-like and indistinct. All at once I splashed into the water. Water was in front of us, so we turned to the left. There was water, too. And water was behind us.

"We're nabbed," I says to Mark; "we've run out on a point of land."

Well, sir, it did look as if we were goners. All Collins and Jiggins had to do was come and get us. But they hadn't discovered the little peninsula yet and were wallowing around maybe a hundred feet off.

Mark was moving around slow and cautious. Finally I heard him sort of chuckle. "Here's the boat," he whispered. "I thought this was like the place your uncle said it would be."

We were as quiet as could be getting to where it was, but Collins and Jiggins heard us and yelled. We jumped into the boat and started to push off, but before we were away from the shore Collins loomed up out of the murkiness and grabbed at the stern.

"I got you," he said, business-like as anything. Somehow I didn't like the sound of his voice.

He missed us first grab and took a step into the water. Just as he reached for us again the most unearthly sound I ever heard came wavering over the water. It was a horrid kind of a sound. A mysterious, shuddery sound that made you draw all together and wish you were in the house by a warm fire.

"Ha-ha-ha! Ha-ha-ha-ha! Ha-ha-ha-ha-ha-ha!" it came. Weird? Why, weird was no name for it! It was the craziest, awfulest laugh in the world. Collins stopped and straightened up like he'd been shot.

"Shove," says Mark, who wasn't so scared but he could take advantage of what was going on. I was almost paralyzed, and so were Plunk and Tallow, but we shoved, and the boat glided off out of Collins's reach.

Then came that laugh once more. "Ha-ha! Ha-ha-ha-ha-ha! Ha-ha-ha-ha!" It was half laugh and half shriek. All of it was crazy—plum lunatic crazy.

"What is it?" I whispered. I couldn't have spoken out loud to save my neck.

Mark chuckled. "Git to r-r-rowin'," says he.

We did.

"But what's making that noise?" I asked.

Before the words were out of my mouth the laugh came shrieking at us again.

"Sounds awful, don't it?" says Mark.

"Let's git out of this," says Tallow. "Something's loose. I don't like it."

Mark chuckled again. Then he started to laugh so he shook all over.

"Well," I says, as mad as could be, "what's so funny about it?"

"Don't you know what that l-l-laugh was?" he asked back at me.

"If I did," says I, "maybe I wouldn't be so all-fired scared."

"Likely not," he says. "The thing that made that laugh is the craziest thing in the world, folks say. When you w-w-want to tell how c-c-crazy a person is you say it's as crazy as the th-th-th-thing that's making that laugh."

# CHAPTER VI

We sat there in the boat about a hundred feet from shore and watched Collins and the fat man floundering around on the bank. We could just see them, but gradually it got lighter and lighter until we could make them out as plainly as they could us. Most of the time Mark was laughing to himself.

"What you laughing at?" I asked him.

"At the way we r-r-ran," says he.

"It wasn't any laughin'-matter," says I.

"You don't think they'd have h-h-hurt you, do you?"

"I don't think anything else."

"Shucks!" says he. "They only come after us l-l-like they did because they were s-s-startled. We s-s-scared 'em."

"And they scared us," I says, sharp-like.

"They might 'a' mauled us a l-l-little," says Mark, "but nothin' more."

"Well," says Plunk, "what we goin' to do now?"

"Nothin' for a bit," says Mark. "When they clear out we'll go home."

"But what we goin' to do about what we heard?" Tallow wanted to know.

Mark looked disgusted. "Why," says he, as sarcastic as could be, "we're g-g-goin' to write it down on paper and b-b-bury it where nobody can ever f-find it."

Collins and Jiggins had been sitting with their heads together while we talked. Just after Mark got through speaking Collins came close to the water and yelled at us.

"Hey, fellows," says he, pleasant-like, "come on a-shore. What ails you, anyhow?"

"N-n-nothin'," says Mark. "We're sittin' here, gittin' ready to f-f-f-fish."

"What made you run when we came?"

"What made you chase us?"

"That was just for fun. We thought maybe we'd scare you."

"You did," says Mark.

"We knew you were hiding down there. That's why Jiggins and I made that joke in the wagon. We knew we'd get you all excited."

"What joke?" Mark asked, with his face as dumb and foolish as a pumpkin lantern.

"Didn't you hear what we said?" I could see Collins was beginning to feel relieved.

"I hain't heard no j-j-joke this morning," says Mark.

Collins turned to Jiggins and said, low, but not so low we couldn't hear him across the water, "There, I told you they couldn't have heard."

"I ain't so sure," says Jiggins, looking hard at Mark. "That fat kid don't appear to me like his ears were wadded with cotton."

Collins shrugged his shoulders. "They wouldn't understand if they did hear," he says. "They're only kids."

Jiggins snorted. "I guess, friend Collins," says he, "you don't know much about boys." With that he got up and started back toward the wagon. "Come on," says he, emphatic-like. "We got something to do, and we got to do it quick."

Collins turned and laughed and called good-by to us; then he followed after Jiggins. Mark was laughing again.

"Now what?" I asked him. He was always seeing things to laugh at none of the rest of us saw, and sometimes it made me a little mad.

"They're goin' to be d-d-disappointed again," says he. "Jiggins is headin' for Uncle Hieronymous."

It was funny. There the fat man was hurrying off to uncle's cabin so he could get there and buy his mineral rights before we could come to warn him. And when he got there uncle would be somewhere else. It didn't look as if the firm of Jiggins & Collins was having very much good luck.

"Let 'em go," says I. "It may do them good, and they can't do any harm."

"They might get track of your uncle," says Tallow.

"I dun'no' how," says I. "Nobody knows where he is but us fellows. If they knew what he was gone for it wouldn't be very easy to find him."

"Just the s-s-same," says Mark, "we got to f-find him, and we mustn't lose any t-t-time about it."

"How'll we do it?" I asked.

"I dun'no' now," says he, "but I'll think it out. Let's s-s-start for home."

We rowed the boat to shore and fastened it; then we started for Uncle Hieronymous's cabin. I own up I felt sort of shaky about going back there just then, for there wasn't a doubt Jiggins and Collins were there, but Mark said there wasn't any danger, so along we went. I guess Tallow and Plunk figured the same way I did, and that was to think no fat boy in Michigan could show he had more nerve than I did.

Sure enough, the men were there, sitting on the doorstep, when we turned the corner into the clearing. Mark never even hesitated, so we kept right at his heels.

"Hello!" says he. "What you d-d-doin' here?"

"Came to see Mr. Bell," says Collins. "He seems to be out."

Jiggins was screwing his face around as if he didn't like things very well. All of a sudden he shook a pudgy finger at Mark and said, "Young feller, if you know as much as you look as if you *don't* know, King Solomon could take lessons in law of you."

Mark let on he didn't understand, but I knew he was tickled. It always tickled him to have folks let on they thought he was smart. *He* thought he was smart, all right, though he never was disagreeable about it.

"I dun'no' nothin' about law," he said, as vacant as a deserted house. "What d'you mean about Solomon?"

"Huh!" snorted Jiggins.

"Where's your uncle?" Collins asked me.

"He hain't got back yet," I told him.

"Hasn't got back from where?"

"Why," says I, trying to make out I was as imbecile-like as Mark let on to be—"why, from where he went to."

"Can you beat that?" Collins says to Jiggins, and his face was funny to look at. "What is this, anyhow? A home for the feeble-minded?"

Jiggins began to sing to himself—a way he had, I found out afterward, when he was provoked or thinking hard. "Diddle-dee-dum," says he, in a squawky voice. "Diddle-dee-dum. Diddle-diddle-dum-dum." Then he stopped sudden and asked, "When's he coming back?"

"D-d-don't b'lieve he's comin' to-night," says Mark.

"It isn't any use," Collins says to Jiggins. "They don't know, or if they do they haven't got brains enough to tell. Though where their brains went to I don't know. Last time I saw them they seemed to have plenty."

"They did, eh?" says Jiggins, sharp-like. "Oh-ho, they did, eh? Um. Him. Diddle-diddle-dee. Diddle-dee-dee-dum." And he went on singing for a couple of minutes. "Look here, young feller," says he to Mark, "you ain't fooling me. I'm onto you, and don't you forget it. I take off my hat to you, I do. All the way off." He turned to Collins. "I'd give a dollar," says he, "to know what that kid'll be when he grows into a man."

Now when you come to think of it that was a sort of a compliment.

"Come on," says Collins. "We might as well get along. When your uncle comes back tell him we just dropped in. It wasn't anything important. Just visiting."

"I'll tell him," says I.

They turned and went off. As they got to the road Jiggins stopped and twisted his pudgy head on his fat neck to look at us again, and he had the sort of expression a boy wears just before he sticks out his tongue. If he hadn't been a man I bet he would have stuck out his tongue. Somehow that made me mad, and right then and there I did the biggest fool thing I ever expect to do in my life.

"Ho!" I yelled. "Think you're smart, don't you? Well, we heard you in that wagon, all right, and we know where uncle is. You needn't think you can smouge him while we're around. We're goin' to go to him as quick as we can and tell—" Then Mark clapped his hand over my mouth, and all of a sudden I knew what I'd done.

"Git into the h-h-house, quick!" he stuttered. "Q-q-quick!"

Both Collins and Jiggins were coming toward us on the run. We didn't wait, but went pell-mell through the door and slammed it after us. Mark locked it. Then he looked at me.

"Binney," says he, slow and deliberate and cutting, "if I had a yaller dawg that didn't know b-b-b-better than to d-d-do sich a thing I'd s-s-skin him and use his h-h-hide for a r-r-rope to hang him with."

I didn't have a word to say, and I can tell you I felt pretty mean. Who wouldn't, I'd like to know? Just by being fresh I'd got us all into a peck of trouble that nobody could see the end of, and maybe fixed it so Collins and Jiggins would get uncle's mine, after all. I felt like crying.

Collins or Jiggins pounded on the door, but it was Collins who called to us to open. We didn't say a word, just kept perfectly quiet. We could hear them talking outside, but couldn't make out what they said.

"Will they bust in?" Plunk asked, his teeth already beginning to chatter.

"'Tain't l-likely," says Mark. "What good would it d-d-do them? Eh? Well, folks with sense don't g-g-generally do things unless there's some g-good to be got out of it."

"What'll we do?" This was Tallow.

"Looks like we'll stay right here."

Collins pounded on the door again. "Tell us where your uncle is," says he, "and we won't hurt you."

"You won't h-h-hurt us, anyhow," says Mark.

"Where is he?"

"He's where you won't ever find him," I says.

"Guess we'll wait for him, then. Maybe you won't like staying in the house till he comes. Might get hungry, eh?" I know he was thinking of Mark when he said that.

"J-just what I thought," says Mark. "It was their only chance. They're g-g-g-going to keep us shut up so's we c-c-can't git to Binney's uncle to warn him."

"Yes," says I, "but s'pose he comes home and finds them besiegin' us? What then? We could holler to him."

Mark sniffed. "'Twon't take m-more than one of them to guard us. The other can g-g-go lookin' for Uncle Hieronymous."

"But they'd never find him," says I.

"P-p-pickles," stuttered Mark, as disgusted as could be.

We all crowded to the window and looked out. I half expected to see the men getting ready to batter down the door, but Mark was right, after all. They weren't doing anything violent, and they didn't look as if they would. That was some comfort. Collins was standing with his back to us, talking to Jiggins, who sat on the ground with his back to a tree. We could hear him singing all the time in that funny way of his: "Dum-diddle-diddle-dee-diddle," and so on. It made you want to throw something at him. After a while they agreed on something, and Collins started out of the clearing.

"Wonder where he's going?" Tallow says.

"S-s-supplies," says Mark. "The enemy's goin' to settle down for a s-s-siege."

There he was off at a game again. It didn't seem to matter what came up, Mark had to pretend something. This time we found out we were a party of explorers who had run onto a mysterious tribe of white men in the middle of Africa. These white men didn't want to be discovered at all, so they were after us hot and heavy. We'd made a bully fight, Mark said, but there were too many of them for us, so we sought refuge in a cavern where they could come at us only one at a time.

"We g-g-got to sell our lives dear," says Mark.

"Can't we make a rush for it?" I suggested.

"'Twouldn't be no use. There's th-th-thousands of 'em all around us. You d-don't think they'd let us g-git away with the s-s-sacred jewel, do you?"

"Oh," says I, "we got the sacred jewel, did we? I thought we were chased out before we got hands on it."

Mark shook his head and then wagged it from side to side. I really think he believed what he said and thought for the minnit that we were really what we were playing we were.

"No," says he, puffed-up-like, and proud as a pigeon. "While you fellows was fightin' 'em off I made a g-g-grab for the jewel and got it. See!" He held up a white door-knob he'd found some place. "It'll make us all rich," says he, "maybe—who knows? But if we take it to some king or queen or somethin' they'll m-m-make dukes or e-earls of us."

"Bully," says Plunk. "I want to be a markiss."

"You're m-more like to git burned at the stake," says Mark.

We took another peek out of the window. Jiggins was still sitting under his tree, not ten feet from the door, and it did look as if his eyes were shut.

"Hus-ss-sh!" whispered Mark. "Maybe we can git the door open and sneak out. If we can g-g-git to the canoe we're all right. Then we can p-p-paddle downstream till we find your uncle. Still, n-n-now."

We edged to the door quiet and drew the bolt. Mark went first. He opened it a teeny crack, then a little more. He was just ready to pull it way back when Jiggins up and sort of chuckled.

"I been expectin' some caper," says he. "Now you git back into the house like good boys. We don't aim to hurt you any, but we can't have you rampaging around the country. 'Twouldn't do, now, would it? If you were me you wouldn't stand for it, would you? 'Course not. Now go on back and behave."

"How long we got to stay cooped up here?" I asked him, sharp-like.

"Well," says he, "that depends. You see, Mr. Collins and me have business with your uncle. From what I heard you yell a spell back there's something you want to tell him. Did I hear right? I shouldn't be a mite surprised if I did. Um. Well, Mr. Collins and me we don't want any bad impressions given. Not we. We want folks to think well of us. If you was to tell your uncle what you want to tell him it ain't likely he'd have anything to do with Mr. Collins and me—now, is it?" Then he began to sing again, "Diddle-diddle-de-dum-diddle-dee."

He did seem like a jolly sort of fat man. I liked Collins, too. Even after I found out he was trying to get Uncle Hieronymous's mine away from him I couldn't help liking him. The other fellows told me afterward they felt a whole lot the same way I did. Somehow I never could believe they were very bad men. They wouldn't have stolen anything or hurt anybody. But, Mark says, they figgered out this was a business deal that they were getting the best of. Lots of folks can't see just honest when their business is mixed up in what they do.

"You're beat, anyhow," I says to him. I didn't say it mean, but just as if I believed it.

"Maybe so," says he. "Maybe so, but we hain't given up yet."

"We'll git away," says Tallow.

"More'n likely," says he, "but Collins and me we'll do our best to keep you."

"What if Uncle Hieronymous should come and find you keepin' us pris'ners?" says I. "He'd sort of suspect somethin', wouldn't he?"

"I calc'late he would, now. But Collins and me we hain't aiming to let him discover us keeping you prisoners. One of us is going to find him."

"Huh!" says I. "You can't do it."

"Maybe not," says he. "Can't never tell. But we'll try. Now, boys, go on back in the house like I said. I don't want to get harsh with you, not a mite. But you got to mind."

We went. Once inside, and Mark locked the door again.

"We want to look out for that fat man," says he. "He's cunnin'. You can't f-f-fool him easy. Don't you think you can."

"I don't think anything about it," says I. "Now let's git somethin' to eat. I'm starvin'."

# CHAPTER VII

You may think it would be an easy thing to sneak out of Uncle Hieronymous's cabin without being seen. To anybody who doesn't know just how things were it would seem as if there wouldn't be any trouble about it at all, but there was, just the same. In the first place, the cabin was little—only three rooms. All the door there was opened out of the back, and the two men were guarding that. On the side of the cabin at the right of the door there wasn't a window, and there was only one at the end opposite. There were two windows on the left-hand side and one alongside the door. This was the window uncle used to feed Martha and Mary through. You see right away there were two sides we couldn't get out of—the one with no windows in it and the one where the door was. As soon as Collins came back they fixed the back end so we couldn't escape there, and it wasn't any trick at all—they just nailed the window down on the outside.

"Collins n-n-never thought of that," says Mark Tidd. "It was the f-f-fat feller."

"Huh!" I grunted, because I knew just what he was thinking. He had it all figured out. Jiggins must be smart just because he was fat. "I guess skinny folks has some brains," I says.

"Anyhow," says he, "these folks have f-f-fixed it so we're goin' to have to use our b-b-brains to git out. Let's think things over."

He sat down and began pulling at his fat cheek the way he always does when he's studying hard, and his little eyes were almost shut. But you should have seen how they twinkled—what you could see of them. The other three of us sat down and thought too, but nobody seemed to have much luck at it.

"The s-s-savages," says Mark, "have stopped up one openin' to this c-c-cavern." He meant the end where Jiggins nailed down the window. "Then," says he, "there's nothin' but solid rock on that s-s-side. If we g-g-git out it must be through the reg'lar openin' [he meant the door] or over on th-th-this side. But," says he, "they're w-w-watchin' there."

Just then we heard a hammering, and when we looked there was Jiggins nailing up the windows on the left side.

Mark shook his head and acted like he was actually proud of Jiggins. "That's what I'd 'a' d-d-done myself," says he. "Now we got to g-g-git out right at that end where they're w-w-watchin'."

We all went to the back window and looked out.

"It's goin' to be a reg'lar siege," I says, for Collins was just putting up a little tent.

"They'll never let us g-git away with the jewel," says Mark; and he took that old door-knob out of his pocket and looked at it as if it was worth a million dollars.

The tent wasn't a regular tent. It was just a square of canvas. Collins stretched a rope between two small trees that grew about ten feet from the door and threw his canvas over it. Then he staked down the edges and had a good shelter to sleep in.

"How many s-s-savages do you count?" Mark asked.

"Two," says Tallow, without thinking.

"Two!" snorted Mark. "You must be b-b-blind. I see two war parties with fifty in each of th-them. That makes a hundred, don't it?"

"Sure," says Tallow. "I wasn't thinkin'."

"If we d-d-don't git out 'fore night," says Mark, "I got a scheme for givin' 'em a s-scare, anyhow."

"What is it?" Plunk wanted to know; but Mark wouldn't tell him. Mark always was that way. If he had a plan he wouldn't tell it to a soul till he had to. I guess he was naturally good at keeping a secret. You couldn't get anything out of him he didn't want to tell if you offered him the Wicksville bank and all the money in it.

"Let's th-th-think of dinner," says Mark. "It's twelve o'clock. We haven't eaten f-f-for two hours."

Collins and Jiggins were cooking their dinner over a fire outside. They saw us looking out at them, and Jiggins called:

"Not hungry, boys? Oh no! Certainly not! If your appetites get to stirring around let us know. You will, won't you? To be sure."

"We c-can lend you some c-c-canned stuff," says Mark, "if you haven't all you n-need."

That sort of made Collins's face fall, but Jiggins went on grinning.

"No matter," says he. "Can't starve you out, eh? Don't care. Keep you shut up, just the same. Can't get out, eh? Windows stuck. Stuck tight. How d'you s'pose that happened?"

"I c-c-could tell you somethin' else to do," says Mark, "but I guess I won't."

"What's that? What's that?" Jiggins was paying attention. You could see by his face he had considerable respect for Mark. "Guess I'll study over it a bit," says he. "Study does it. Sure." Then he began singing his tune again, "Tee-dum-dee. Deedle-deedle-dum."

"There's a way to do everything," says Mark, "even to get out of this cabin."

"To be sure," says Jiggins. "No doubt. But find it, my boy. Find it. That's the difficulty, eh? Easy to say, not easy to do."

We went back in the other room after we had our dinner, and Mark read to us out of a book he had in his satchel. It was a dandy book, and the name of it was *Kidnapped*. There was a fellow in it by the name of Alan Breck who was a hummer. I liked him better than I did the real hero of the book, who seemed to me to be a dumb-headed sort of fellow. Maybe that was because he was Scotch. Plunk Smalley is Scotch, and sometimes we have the hardest time getting things into his head.

There wasn't anything else to do, so we read all the afternoon, taking turns. Mark said the same man who wrote that book was the author of a lot more. Right there I made up my mind I'd read every one of them, and so did the other fellows.

You'd be surprised to hear how quickly the afternoon went past. If ever you have a dull day on your hands just get a book by that man; his name is Stevenson; and—well, there's no use telling about it, you never will understand until you do it.

We didn't even want to stop for supper, but Mark said it was our duty to eat. Maybe it was; anyhow, nobody ever heard of Mark Tidd shirking that particular sort of duty.

After we were through Mark had Tallow get on a chair and haul down a long cane fish-pole Uncle Hieronymous had laying across nails driven in the wall. He took his knife and cut off the small end.

"What you doin'?" I asked him. "Maybe uncle wants that pole."

"Calc'late," says he, "your uncle would want his mine worse. Wouldn't he?"

I didn't answer back, but stood and watched to see what he was up to. When he had the pole cut off he went into the kitchen and got the knife uncle used to clean fish. It was a heavy knife, and sharp. Why, you could have shaved with it, I bet.

"Git some st-st-strong twine," says Mark to me.

I rummaged around until I found a whole ball of it. Mark took it as calm as could be without even saying "much obliged." Then what should he do but begin to lash the fish-knife to the end of the fish-pole. All the time he never said a word. He was that way always—liked to get you all worked up and curious. If you asked a question he wouldn't tell you a thing. He was almost mean about it.

When he had the knife fastened he laid the whole thing down on the floor. It looked like a spear. From one end to the other it was about twenty feet long, and I'll bet any savage would have been glad to get hold of it, for it would have been a weapon like he never imagined.

"Goin' to spear 'em?" Tallow asked.

"Nope," says Mark; "this is to k-k-kill mosquitoes."

We knew it wasn't any use to bother him any more. He'd tell us about it when he was ready, and not a minnit before. It didn't matter how mad we got. When he took it into his head the time to tell had come he'd tell, and horses couldn't drag it out of him before.

"I don't see any sense to it," I told him, because I thought possibly I could make him mad and so get him to tell, but it didn't work.

"You ain't expected to," was all he said.

We lighted the lamp and read some more *Kidnapped*. Mosquitoes were buzzing around, and a couple of times I felt like telling Mark it was time to begin on them with his spear, but I didn't. Sometimes it's safer not to make remarks to him. He's fat and he stutters, but that doesn't keep him from thinking as quickly as anybody else. The fellow that goes monkeying with Mark Tidd is apt to get a little better than he gives.

Once or twice Mark got up to look out of the window at the camp of the enemy. "The f-f-fat chief is on guard," he says. "I can't see the thin one. Maybe he's layin' in a-a-ambush in case we t-t-try to make a rush."

Another time he reported: "They've g-got a smudge to keep off mosquitoes. Bet they're bitin' out there."

"Wonder if they'll keep guard all night?" asked Tallow.

Mark just looked at him. Then he says, sarcastic-like: "Naw; 'course not. They know we're afraid of the d-d-dark, don't they? What's the use of keepin' g-g-guard?"

The third time he went to the window he stayed quite a while.

"What is it?" I asked.

He motioned with his hand for me to keep quiet; then in a few minnits he came back and sat down without a word.

"What was going on?" Plunk wanted to know.

"I guess the f-f-fat chief has turned in. The thin one is k-keeping watch." You see, it had to be a game all the time. What was actually going on wasn't enough for Mark. If we really were besieged by white savages in the middle of Africa with a big jewel in our hands that we'd stolen, he would have up and played we were in a cabin up near the source of the Père Marquette River, watched by a couple of men who wanted to keep us from warning Uncle Hieronymous. I never could see the sense to a lot of his games, but, after all, we had a lot of fun. Not as much as he did, though.

"It's dark," says Mark. Then he grinned at us and looked at his spear. "'Most time to git after those m-m-mosquitoes," says he.

He picked up the spear and looked careful at the way the knife was fastened onto the end of it; then he felt of the edge of the knife to be sure it was sharp. All this time he never said a word, though he knew we were so interested we could hardly keep from rolling off our chairs onto the floor.

"Wonder if I c-c-could git up into the attic?" he says.

In the dining-room ceiling was a square place to get up into the loft, but there wasn't any way to reach it.

"Wish we had a step-ladder," says I.

"Might as well w-w-wish for a pair of st-st-stairs," says he. "We got to find some other way."

We left it to him; he was better than we were at finding ways; and, most likely, if one of us had found a way he wouldn't have used it, no matter how good it was. He was pretty fond of thinking up things himself. He liked to astonish folks.

Not that this was very difficult. All he did was have the table moved under the opening and a chair put on it. By standing on the chair it was easy for an ordinary boy to get up into the loft. It wasn't quite so easy for Mark, but he got around that part of it by piling a box on the seat of the chair and getting on top of that. When he stood there his shoulders were through the opening. He got his arms in and began to wriggle through. It was a tight fit, and there's no doubt it was mighty funny to watch. Mark wriggled and squirmed. His legs thrashed around and sawed the air, but he kept at it. He grunted and groaned and tugged and pulled. For a while it looked as though he was too big for the hole and would stick in it till we hauled him down by the legs, but after ten minutes of hard work he pushed and hunched himself up.

For a while he sat with his legs dangling and panted. When he was rested he called down to us, cautious-like, and says: "Pass up the spear. And k-keep quiet. One of you c-can come up. The others better s-s-sneak to the back window and watch. But keep still. D-don't breathe."

I was up on the table and half through the hole before the other fellows had a chance to object, so they had to go to the back window.

Mark crawled to the back of the house, careful and slow. You had to be careful, whether you wanted to or not, because there wasn't any floor—just joists with lath and plaster between. I followed him as close as I could. There was a little window about a foot square that overlooked the tent where the enemy were, and Mark was making for it.

"Wonder if it'll c-c-come out?" he whispered.

"Dun'no'," says I.

We tried it, but it didn't seem to want to open. Mark studied it awhile and fussed around with it. It was hot and dusty and uncomfortable up there, and I hoped he would be able to let a bit of air in before long. Just then the window gave with a little creak, and came back in Mark's hands.

"Whee!" he whispered. "Now p-pass me the spear."

I handed it to him and he poked it out of the window a little at a time, not making a sound. I didn't know what he was up to, but somehow the darkness and the stillness and one thing and another made me so excited I could hardly breathe. I crowded as close to Mark as I could and looked over his shoulder. I could see the tent below us, with Collins leaning against a tree not five feet away from it. Mark didn't move, but just held out his fish-pole spear and waited.

After quite a while Collins got up and went over to the tent. He stooped and reached inside. It looked as if he couldn't reach what he wanted, so he crawled in careful-like, so as not to wake Jiggins. Mark chuckled.

Then he reached out with the knife on the end of his fish-pole and brought it down kersnap on the rope that held up the tent. The rope was tight, and the knife was sharp. He didn't have to whack it again. We could hear the rope snap; then the tent just sort of plumped down on Collins and Jiggins. Mark hauled in his spear quick, and we waited to see what would happen. A lot did happen quick.

We could see a floundering and flapping around under the canvas. Collins let out a startled yell. Jiggins was waked up suddenly, and didn't like it very well, I guess, for he yelled, too. Then the canvas began to roll and jump and wabble in the funniest way you ever saw. Both men yelled and hollered and kicked and thrashed around until Jiggins got his head out at one end. I laughed out loud when I saw him crawl from under. He looked as though he'd been trying to butt through a cy-clone, and he looked scared. In a minnit Collins worked out of the other end. They just looked at each other.

"*You* put up that tent," said Jiggins. "You did. Of course you did. Nobody else." He was mad clear through.

"What made it come down?" Collins asked, bewildered-like.

They both walked over to the nearest tree and felt of the rope. Jiggins pulled the loose end to him and looked at it. He chuckled, and his chuckle sounded sort of like Mark's.

"Should have known better," he said. "Fat boy. Nobody's fool. Might have known. Snipped the rope. Don't know how. He found a way. Look out for that boy. Look out for him, eh? You bet."

He turned toward the house and grinned. "You're all right, fat kid," says he. "That scores one for you."

Mark and I started to get down again. I managed all right, but he had quite a time of it. When we were down we went to the back window with Plunk and Tallow. Collins and Jiggins were moving their tent about ten feet farther from the house.

"Well," says I to him, "that was fun, all right, but what good did it do?"

He pointed to the tent. "It m-moves them another t-ten feet away," says he. "That may be important p-p-pretty soon."

# CHAPTER VIII

It was time for us to go to bed, but Mark called us into the dining-room to a council of war. We sat down around the table, with Mark at the head. He started talking almost in a whisper.

"S-s-speak low," says he. "We don't want the enemy to overhear our plans."

That was right, for they might have sneaked up to the side of the house to listen. Mark wasn't the sort of fellow to neglect any precaution just because it might not be necessary. Sometimes I thought he was too cautious, but usually it turned out he did the right thing.

"We can't g-git out of here by daylight," he says. "It's got to be at n-n-night or early in the morning. Morning's the best time, 'cause folks are t-t-tired with watchin'. 'Bout three in the m-mornin'."

"You seem pretty sure we're goin' to git out," says I.

"We *got* to git out," says he, just as if that settled it. It didn't seem to enter his head that sometimes folks can't do things they think they've got to do.

"All right," says I, but I was feeling sort of hopeless. "Let's git at it. We're losin' time."

"We w-won't lose any more," Mark says. "Has your uncle got a shovel?"

"I dun'no'," says I; "and if he has it's out in the barn."

"Then we g-g-got to make one."

"How?"

"Out of a board. Whittle it. We better make a c-couple while we're at it."

There was a big soap-box in the kitchen that Uncle Hieronymous used for a sort of table. Mark decided this would do all right, so we pulled it apart, and he and I set to work whittling shovels out of it. They were pretty clumsy, but Mark said they were all right, and so long as they suited him they were good enough for me.

"N-n-now," says he, "we want a hatchet."

"It's in the cupboard," says I. "What you want of it?"

"P-p-pry up a board in the floor," says he.

"You can't crawl out under the house. There isn't any opening. The logs go down to the ground all the way around."

"I knew it," he says. "What you s'pose the sh-sh-shovels are for?"

I got the hatchet, and we decided it was best to pull up a board in the kitchen, where they were wider. The kitchen floor was rough lumber, and some boards were eight inches wide, with cracks between.

"It'll make a n-noise," says Mark, "and they'll suspect we're up to somethin'." He thought a minnit, pulling hard on his cheek. Then he got down the dish-pan and handed it to Plunk and gave Tallow a couple of milk-pans.

"When we b-begin work," says he, "you make a racket. Keep at it steady." All of a sudden he looked disgusted and kind of sorry for himself. He shook his head and slapped his leg. "There," says he, "I almost forgot the window. Hang a quilt over it, Binney, so's they can't see in."

I did that, and then we went to work on the floor, but first I told Mark I had a better noise-maker than a tin pan. I got it out of my satchel. It was a tin can with a string through it. There was a piece of resin, too, and when you put the can against a window and pulled the string it let out a racket that would scare a crow. Tallow took that and started in. Plunk pounded on the pans. All of us war-whooped.

It was hard work getting up the board, and we made a lot of noise at it, but I don't believe Jiggins and Collins ever noticed anything besides the squealing squawk of the tin can and the banging on the pans and the hollering. It must have surprised them some, and I bet they wondered what we were up to. At last we got two boards up. That gave us plenty of space to crawl through.

Mark signaled to Tallow and Plunk to let up their racket. My, but it sounded quiet when they stopped! You never know how quiet stillness is until a big noise stops all of a sudden. Collins began to yell outside.

"Hey!" says he, "what you kids doing? Think this is the Fourth of July?"

"We were j-j-just trying to keep from f-fallin' asleep," says Mark.

Collins laughed. It wasn't a mad laugh, but a really-truly good-natured one. "I hope you'll get through before I go off watch. It's rather company for me while I'm up, but most likely my friend Jiggins won't appreciate it."

"He don't," came a sleepy voice. "Not any. Decidedly not. First, down comes tent. Second, hullabalee. Quit it. Quit it."

"G-guess we will," says Mark. "Good night."

They both called good night, friendly-like. It hardly seemed we were prisoners and they were enemy, but all the same that was the fact. I've heard about pickets in the Civil War meeting between the lines and exchanging things and being good friends, only to try to shoot each other next morning, and it didn't seem exactly possible. I couldn't see how a man you liked could be your enemy and how you could try to beat him, but I do now.

Mark wiggled his finger at us, and we gathered in a little knot around him, with our heads close together.

"We'll divide into two w-watches," he stuttered. "Binney and I will w-w-watch first. Two hours. Then Tallow and Plunk. By mornin' we must have it d-d-dug."

"Have what dug?"

"The tunnel," says Mark. "We're prisoners in Andersonville, hain't we? D-d-didn't the rebels capture us, and hain't we starvin'? I'd like to know if we hain't. Look out of the window and you c-can see gray-coated guards with m-muskets."

Here was a surprise. We weren't shut into a cave by white savages any longer. We didn't have any jewel out of an idol. We were nothing but Union soldiers in a rebel prison.

"Binney and I will d-dig two hours," Mark says. "Then we'll wake you. You d-dig two hours and wake us. It's got to be d-d-done before daylight."

Plunk and Tallow went to bed with their clothes on while Mark and I put out the light and crowded under the floor. There was plenty of room when we got down, but it was dark as a pocket. Mark lighted the lantern.

"Won't they see that?" I asked.

"No," says he. "There hain't no ch-chinks."

We crawled to the front of the house and began to dig with our wooden shovels. The digging was easy because the house sat on a regular sand-pit. All that country is sand, anyhow. Mark says it was probably the shore of Lake Michigan once, and that the lake kept throwing up sand and throwing up sand until it crowded itself back fifty miles or so. Maybe that is so, but it took a mighty long time to do it.

The worst part of the digging was the way sand kept running back into the hole. We couldn't stop it, and so we had to dig about four times as much as we would if it had only stayed where it belonged. We never rested, though, and by the end of our two hours we had a good deep hole dug. We'd got below the logs. Plunk and Tallow would have to make the hole larger and begin to tunnel under. It looked to me as if we could finish all right in our second two hours. That would bring us out about three o'clock.

I slept like a log until Tallow waked me up. It didn't seem as though I'd got my head down on the pillow, and for a minnit I didn't want to get up. I didn't care if we never escaped. But Tallow kept on shaking me and yanking me till I was roused, and then it was all right. Mark and I went under the house again, and I want to say that Tallow and Plunk had worked like beavers. They'd done a lot more than I expected they would. Mark was tickled, too.

"Now," says he, "we got to work f-f-fast."

We did. The dirt flew. We found out, though, that tunneling in sand isn't all it might be cracked up to be. The digging is easy, but the roof don't stay up. I had my head and shoulders through under the logs tunneling away while Mark took my sand and threw it out of the hold. Maybe I went at it too hard, or maybe it would have done what it did, anyhow, but all of a sudden the whole roof gave way and came down onto me kerplunk. It buried my head and arms and shoulders, and I want to stop right here to say that I was the scairtest boy in the state of Michigan.

I thought I was a goner. I couldn't breathe or holler or anything. The sand was so heavy I couldn't move, and I guess if Mark hadn't been right there to see what was going on I'd have smothered, sure. He didn't waste any time, though, but grabbed me by the feet and yanked me out a-kiting. I was full of sand—eyes, mouth, ears— and it was a couple of minnits before I could force myself back to work. But I did, and Mark patted me on the back. That made me feel pretty good, I tell you.

From then on there wasn't any tunneling to speak of. All we had to do was clear out the sand that had caved in. In an hour we had a hole big enough to crawl through, and only had to tear out the sod that hadn't caved in to get out. It was half past two by Mark's watch. We crept back to the loose boards and got into the house again.

It was hard to wake Tallow and Plunk, but we did.

"You f-f-fellows have got to stay here," says Mark. "Binney and I will g-go. Binney's got a right to go 'cause it's his u-uncle, and I got to go to l-look after things."

There wasn't any argument about that.

"Jiggins and C-Collins mustn't discover we've gone for a l-long time," says Mark. "You two have g-g-got to act like four. Make 'em think we're all h-here. Understand?"

"Sure," says Tallow and Plunk.

"And when they f-f-find out, don't tell which way we went."

"What d'you take us for?" Tallow says.

"We'll git back as s-s-soon as we can," Mark told them. "But maybe it'll be a w-week."

"We'll be all right," says Plunk.

Mark turned to me. "Git that p-pail of paint," he says, "and the brush. I'll carry the hammer and a paper of tacks and that chunk of c-c-canvas hangin' there."

"What for?" I asked.

"We're goin' in a c-canoe, hain't we?"

"Yes."

"D-down a river we don't know?"

"Yes."

"With stones and d-dead-heads in it?"

"Sure."

"If we hit one of 'em, what'll h-happen?"

"We'll bust the canoe."

"That," says he, "is the reason for the p-p-paint and things."

Now, I never would have thought of that. It was just another example of the way he took precautions and got ready for accidents that might never happen. But don't you ever think he wasn't right this time. If he hadn't brought that mess of stuff we—well, there's no telling what would have happened to us. Anyhow, it was mighty lucky we had it along.

"Come on, Binney," says Mark.

Now that the practical explaining was over, Mark got back to his game of Union prisoners again.

"G-g-good-by, comrades," says he. "I've been chosen to go f-f-first. Maybe I won't never see you again."

He looked like he was going to cry. Maybe you won't think this is so, but when Mark Tidd was pretending anything he pretended so hard he really believed he wasn't pretending at all.

"The next man," says he to me, "will start in f-five minnits if he don't hear the crack of a gun. If he d-d-does he better not come. That will mean I was d-discovered—and killed, most likely." He started through the hole in the floor. "Five minnits," says he, and disappeared. But he poked his head up once more.

"G-gimme the clothes-line," says he.

I handed it to him, and he disappeared for good.

# CHAPTER IX

It was pretty hard to wait five minutes before I started, and it was exciting, too. We were so still it made me nervous, but we just couldn't talk, for we were listening—listening to hear if Mark was discovered. Minute after minute went by, and we didn't hear a sound, so we concluded he had got away safely. At last my time came. I said good-by to the fellows and went through the floor. This time there was no lantern, and I had to crawl under the house in that black darkness. I found the hole, all right. But I would rather have found it some other way, for I fell into it and got my mouth full of sand again. It was lucky the cover of the paint-pail was on tight, or I'd have spilled it.

It was no trick at all to claw through the little tunnel and get out on the other side. It was dark out of doors—dark and cold and lonesome. Around at the front of the house I could hear some one stirring—I don't know whether it was Jiggins or Collins—and that made me pretty careful.

I crept straight back, keeping the house between me and the enemy until I got to some underbrush. I ducked into this and swung around to the direction where the canoe lay. I don't want you to think it was easy to find that path through the bushes that led to the canoe. It wasn't. I came very near to getting lost, but I found where the path began at last and hurried down it, taking all the pains I could to be still. I was making good time, though, because I wanted company. I had all I needed of being alone out there in that woods, and you can believe it, too.

Then all of a sudden something seemed to grab my feet. I let out a yell; I couldn't help it. You'd have yelled, too. As I say, something seemed to grab my feet and knock them out from under me, and I came down with a smash. The paint-pail went end over end, but I hung onto the other things. I was in a regular panic, but for a minnit I was too stunned to get up. Then I heard Mark Tidd's voice.

"S-s-sorry to give you a tumble," says he, "but I had to f-find out."

"Find out what?" I snapped.

"If it would w-work."

"Did you do that?"

"T-tied a piece of rope across the path. Tied th-th-three others farther along. They work f-f-fine."

"Oh," says I, "they work great. They tickle me most to death."

"If we were ch-ch-chased they'd come in handy," says he; and just then we heard Tallow holler loud. "Look out!" says he. "They're comin'. Look out!"

They had heard me fall, I guess, and the yell I couldn't stop.

"Now see what you did," I says to Mark, as I groped for the paint. It was his fault, all right; he should have known better; but I expect he got so interested in his experiment he forgot I might make a racket.

"C-can't be helped now," says he. "Come careful."

We ran as fast as we could. Mark knew where the ropes were, and so we got over them safely, and in a couple of jerks of a lamb's tail we were at the canoe. Mark had it in the water all ready, and we stepped in.

"Shove off," says Mark.

Just as we left the shore we heard a crash and a lot of yelling back at the beginning of the path. Somebody had hit Mark's first man-trap.

"L-lucky I thought of that," says he.

"If you hadn't thought of it we never would have been discovered," says I. I was scratched and bumped and felt pretty cross.

"Paddle," says he.

The stream was narrow there, but deep enough to float a canoe. The current was swift, but it was so dark we couldn't see much where we were going. About all we had to go by was that the shore looked blacker than where there wasn't any shore. One good thing was that there weren't any stones or dead-heads or brush-heaps.

We had to take chances or we would have gone along slow and careful, but luck was with us, I expect, and we didn't have any serious accident. A couple of times we scraped the shore, and once we grounded going around a curve, but on the whole we felt pretty well satisfied. We had got away.

The worst of it was that Jiggins and Collins knew which way we'd gone, and would be able to find we left in a canoe. If it hadn't been for Mark's man-trap they would have had to guess at that, and, as likely as not, would have guessed wrong. Anyhow, we had a start, and it was too dark for them to chase us along the shore. I don't know what happened to the men in that path, but I expect they had a couple more tumbles before they came out where we had hidden the canoe.

We paddled along till daylight, and then we kept on paddling. We figured we were safe now, because Jiggins and Collins were left three hours behind; and, besides, we didn't see how they could possibly chase us. There were several things we didn't know, though. It isn't safe to figure up the score till the last man's out, and we crowed too soon. Uncle Hieronymous's mine was worth too much money for these men to give it up without trying pretty average hard, and I will say for them they did their best.

"All we have to do now," says Mark, "is to k-keep on down-stream until we f-f-find your uncle and Ole and Jerry. They're s-s-somewhere along the river, and we can't miss 'em."

The Middle Branch, I guess I've said before, was nothing but a little stream.

Sometimes it was fifteen feet wide, but very seldom any wider, except once in a great while where the current had worn out a pool at a sharp bend—a place like the one where we rescued Mr. Macmillan's landing-net. There was hardly a place where we could have landed, because the underbrush grew right down to the water's edge so thick it would have been next to impossible to get through it without cutting a path with a hatchet. Once, after we had been out about an hour, we jammed into a pile of brush and logs that clogged the stream. It didn't do any harm, but we had to haul the canoe over the top of it. This took us all of twenty minutes. We didn't think anything of it then, but, if only we had known it, twenty minutes was a lot to waste just then.

Shortly after daylight we came out into the Père Marquette River. That meant the real start of our voyage.

"Aha!" says Mark. "The great river the Indians t-t-told us of. I never thought to l-l-live to see it."

"What's that?" says I.

"I'm Father Marquette," says he.

"Shucks!" says I. "He never got way inland as far as this."

"You can't prove it," says he, "and, anyhow, this is the Mississippi River, hain't it?"

"To be sure," says I, "to be sure."

"It's been a wonderful trip, hain't it?" Mark asked. "Canoein' way down the shore of Lake Michigan from Mackinac? When King Louis hears of what we've d-done he'll be p-pretty tickled, I bet."

"Let's see," says I; "you're buried down Ludington way somewheres, ain't you?"

"There's about a dozen places claims my grave. Er"—he stopped and scowled at me—"I mean will claim it when I'm dead and buried."

"How come they to name this river after you, Father Marquette?" I asked him.

"'Cause I d-discovered it," says he.

There we were getting mixed up. We were pretending we were discovering the Mississippi, and right in the middle of it we forgot and talked about the Père Marquette. The Père part of it means "Father," you know.

The big river was considerable wider than the Middle Branch—maybe seventy feet sometimes—and it was swifter and deeper. Right where we were was a sort of shallow, but even at the far side it was good and deep. It was a hard river to canoe on because it was so irregular about being deep. First the water would be over your head, and next it would be so shallow you'd be scraping on the bottom.

We paddled along until we came to a bend in the river where there was a sand-bar sticking out into the water on the point of the bend.

"There," says Mark; "l-let's git ashore for breakfast. No sign of h-hostile Indians."

"All right," says I. "I'm both willin' and hungry."

So we went ashore. I've told you how the river curved and wriggled. Folks tell me it twists five miles through the country to make one mile ahead. I don't know how near right this is, but it didn't seem to us like any exaggeration when we were floating down. Well, what I meant to say was that when we were on the point we could see up-stream only about a thousand feet, and down-stream not so far as that. It was just like being on the shore of a tiny lake, except that the current kept swishing by so fast.

"Haul the canoe up on the s-sand," says Mark, "so the current won't carry it off."

It was on the lower side of the point, and I pulled it up till its nose was sticking into the underbrush.

"Hush!" says Mark. "Look!"

It startled me, but there was nothing to be afraid of. It was just a big crane flopping his wings and coming down to the water about a hundred feet off.

"G-goin' fishin'," Mark whispered.

The crane lighted in the water about to his knees and stood as quiet as a gatepost, waiting for a fish to swim by where he could grab him in his long bill.

While we watched him another crane came settling down not fifty feet from the first one and stood up as straight and stiff as a soldier. He hardly got placed when three more came down and got into the water up-stream farther toward the bend. That made five.

"Whee!" I whispered to Mark, "I never saw so many together before."

"Hush," he says, and pointed up. There, over the trees, came two more cranes with great wings extended, just sort of floating toward us, and they settled in the water, too.

"Must be a fine place to f-f-fish," says Mark, and at that what should happen but two more cranes who picked out spots in the line.

Before we had done being surprised another came rushing down—he was in a hurry, I guess; and then another, who lit at the far end of the line. It was a pretty sight, I tell you. Eleven big cranes, most as tall as I am, all standing as pompous and stiff and motionless as could be, just as if they were on parade.

"I wouldn't have m-missed it for a quarter," says Mark, and I felt that way too.

We forgot about breakfast, it was so interesting to watch them. Every now and then one of them would dart his head down quick as lightning, there would be a splash in the water, and sometimes you could see the big bird gulping down a little fish. This kept up for maybe twenty minutes.

"L-l-look at the last one," says Mark, all of a sudden.

The bird at the far end of the line didn't act satisfied with things—he sort of fidgeted. Then all at once he spread his wings and began slowly flapping them till their tips touched the river. Up he rose, acting for all the world like a startled girl. The next crane caught the scare, and up he went.

"Whew!" Mark whistled. "Somebody comin'. Haul the boat out of sight. Quick!"

We jumped for the canoe and dragged it into the underbrush and lay down on our stomachs beside it.

"Hostile Indians," says Mark.

I was pretty sure in my mind there were no more hostile Indians in Michigan, but, after all, you can never tell. It was wild enough along there to suit anybody, and there might have been a tribe of red men that somehow had got themselves overlooked. So I made no bones about hiding. Mark hadn't meant real Indians, though. He was still being Father Marquette on the Mississippi.

By the time we were well hid the last crane up and flapped into the air, and then around the bend above us poked the blunt end of a boat—a sort of flatboat— and in the front of it was nobody in the world but Jiggins. Mark pinched my leg. Of course Collins was there, too, and they were paddling for all that was in them. Afterward we found out that was a flatboat built special by Larsen, where Collins and Jiggins were staying, for the very purpose of going down the river.

You can bet we laid pretty still. It seemed like it took that boat an hour to get abreast of the point. Both Jiggins and Collins were keeping their eyes straight ahead of them, though, and there wasn't a bit of danger to us. They simply went sweeping by as fast as they could force their boat, thinking they were chasing us. It almost made me laugh. In another few minutes they went out of sight around the next bend, and I was for jumping out of concealment, but Mark held me down.

"Wait," says he, "till we're s-s-sure."

So we waited maybe five minutes. Then Mark decided it would be all right, so we got up and hauled our canoe out.

"Now what?" says I.

"I dun'no'," says he, shaking his head. "G-guess I better think it over some."

So he sat down in the sand, with his fat legs sticking out ahead of him, and tugged away at his round cheek till it looked like he would pinch a hole in it. First he'd shut his little twinkling eyes, and then he'd open them again.

"Well," says I, after my patience was about worn out, "what about it?"

"They won't n-never suspect we're behind 'em," says he.

"No," says I, "but what about their findin' Uncle Hieronymous? They may git to him any minnit. We don't know but he's only a mile down."

"He's more'n that," says Mark.

"How d'you know?" says I.

"Because," says he, "they couldn't ever get a big scow with a derrick on it up h-h-here." He almost strangled getting out that last word, he stuttered so hard.

He stopped a minnit to get his breath, then he says, "We'll just keep stringin' along b-behind them. Maybe we'll f-find a good chance to s-sneak by after a while. There hain't n-nothin' else we can do," says he, with a sort of dissatisfied grin like a fellow grins when he has to take the best he can get.

"Well," says I, "we better git some breakfast, then."

"You bet," says Mark; and his voice sounded real enthusiastic.

# CHAPTER X

"I dun'no'," says Mark Tidd, while we were building a fire and getting breakfast, "whether it's m-more dangerous to be ahead or b-b-behind the enemy."

"Why?" I asked, for it looked to me like we were a lot less likely to be caught when we were behind.

"Well," says he, "if we're ahead we can always t-try to escape by p-paddlin', but if we're behind and run on to 'em sudden, what can we do? We can't paddle up-stream against this c-current, can we?"

"We'll have to go perty careful and keep our eyes open," I says.

We had some coffee and a little bacon. Mark allowed he felt a lot better when it was down, and I'll admit I wasn't half as worried. Mark says eatin' is one of the most important things there is.

"Why," says he, "the Emperor Napoleon told his folks an army travels on its stomach. What he meant was an army of h-h-hungry men wasn't any good to him at all."

We washed up our coffee-pot and frying-pan and packed things away in the canoe. Then we launched her and started out to follow Collins and Jiggins down the river. If it hadn't been for Mark and his games it wouldn't have been very exciting, but right off he started to be Father Marquette again, and I was Louis Joliet, a fur-trader. As near as I could get at it, Mark was to preach to the Indians and convert them while I was swapping two-cent beads for ten-dollar pelts.

"The f-farther we go," says Mark, "the wilder and savager the natives get. A couple of days from now I b-bet we run into cannibals l-like those that passed in the boat."

Collins and Jiggins had got promoted to cannibals now.

We went cautious, I can promise you. Between being honestly worried about the men ahead of us and being make-believe afraid of Indians we came pretty close to having our hands full. Every time we came to a curve we had to go slow and back water so as not to come swinging around on Jiggins & Co. unexpected, and once or twice when the current was strong we did sweep around kerflip. As luck had it, they weren't there waiting for us, but it would have been just the same if they had.

The current was swift all the time, but sometimes it was swifter than others. Whenever the stream got narrower it crowded the water together so it seemed to shoot through; and then it went so smooth and purring-like it almost frightened you. It acted *strong*. It was lucky we knew a little about a canoe, or we would have tipped over or smashed ashore fifty times. Even as it was we brushed a tree that had toppled into the water and grazed a stump that came just to the surface. If we'd hit that square Mark would have had some use for his canvas and paint.

It began to get hot after a while, and we began to get tired. There isn't anything so tiresome to your back as riding in a canoe when you aren't used to it. I wished Mark would say something about taking a rest, but he didn't. I suppose he was wishing I would. Folks get into lots of trouble, off and on, by being afraid to be the first to give in. All the same, I wasn't going to admit I couldn't stand as much as he could.

Once he saw a sort of dilapidated shanty back a ways from the river, and there was a man standing in front of it. Mark said to go ashore and question him.

"He's a p-peaceful Indian," says Mark. "I can tell by his p-paint."

We ran the canoe to shore and got out. The man walked toward us, and he was funny-looking as all-git-out. With one side of his face he was sort of scowling, and with the other side he came pretty close to grinning good-natured.

"Howdy-do," says Mark; and the man nodded with a jerk.

"F-f-fine day," says Mark.

"If you like it hot," says the man.

"Live here?" asked Mark, polite as could be.

The man scowled harder with the scowling side, and kind of wrinkled up the good-natured side of his face. Then he gave the end of his nose a little twist like he wanted to make sure it wouldn't fly off unbeknownst to him while his mind was taken up with other things. Then he cleared his throat and coughed and scratched his head.

"Wa-al," says he, "I sleep here, and I eat here. Some folks that hain't afraid of stretchin' the truth might go so far's to say I live here. Pers'nally it don't look to me like I done a great amount of livin', so to speak."

"F-f-farm?" asked Mark.

"Don't calc'late to," says the man.

"Well," says Mark, sort of puzzled, "what do you do?"

"Right now, young feller, about all I do is hope. 'Tain't a payin' business, though comfortin'. I calc'late to work a mite and fish a mite and loaf consid'able. Doorin' the fall and winter I hunt some and trap and read up in the papers what happens durin' the summer. Also" —he stopped and twisted his nose again— "also I git so energetic-like that I've been knowed to shove a fish-shanty on to the ice and spear."

"S-s-see many folks goin' down the river?" asked Mark.

"'Tain't what you'd call crowded. No. Couldn't go so far's to say people was jostlin' one another."

"Did you happen to see a b-b-boat with two men go past this mornin'?"

"Fat man that was hummin' and a thin man that was sweatin'?"

"Yes," says Mark.

"Sort of in a hurry?"

"They would 'a' b-been," says Mark.

"Lemme think," says the man. "Now, did I see them men or did I jest imagine I seen 'em? If my dawg 'd 'a' been here he'd 'a' barked at anybody that went by. But he didn't bark. That hain't anythin' to go by, though, 'cause he run off last spring." He stopped again and made like he was studying hard.

"Supposin' they'd stopped and asked me had I seen a couple of boys, one fat and one lean? Would that 'a' been them?"

"I guess it would," says Mark; and you could see he was tickled to death with the man.

"Then," says he, "there can't be no doubt I seen 'em."

"How l-long ago?" asked Mark.

"A perty good-sized nap," says he.

Mark didn't understand any more than I did. "What's that?" he cried.

"Just my way of tellin' time," says the man. "Day's divided into naps. I snooze and wake and snooze and wake. I know how long ago a thing happened by countin' back how many times I been asleep."

"How l-long is a perty good-sized nap?"

"More'n twice as long as a skimpy nap."

That was the best we could get out of him, though Mark tried him a couple of times more.

"Did they stop and ask you about anything?" Mark asked.

"Asked me about two boys."

"What did you t-t-tell 'em?"

"Young feller," says the man, scowling like anything with his left eyebrow, "I judged it best not to state anythin' definite. When folks is huntin' for folks it may be friendly and it may be unfriendly. You might be doin' a favor, or you might not, as the case may be. Them men looked perty anxious, so, thinks I, this here is a time for thinkin' and meditation. Likewise it's a time for bein' sure you don't do nothin' about somethin' you don't know nothin' about. So I was what the newspapers calls non-committal. Big word, eh? I've remembered her nigh two years, and hain't never had no use for her before. Pays to save them words, though. Time always comes for 'em."

"What did you say to them?"

"Says I, 'Gentlemen and strangers, I hain't been app'inted watchman of this here river, though I do notice it consid'able. But I got my weaknesses, gentlemen, and one of 'em is for sleep. I jest woke up, so to speak. Before I done so there might 'a' been a Barnum's Circus parade a-floatin' down, though it would 'a' been the first time sich a thing's happened in ten year.' That's all I said to 'em, young fellers, and they went away in more of a hurry than ever."

"If you w-w-wouldn't tell *them* anything," says Mark, suspicious-like, "what makes you tell *us*?"

The man didn't say a thing for a minnit, and his face got to look the same on both sides. It was a kind of wistful look, I guess. "When it's boys," he says, very slow, "all rules don't work. Boys is— I like boys," says he, and then began again to scowl with one side and look like he didn't care with the other. What he said and the way he said it made you pretty sorry for him, and you didn't know why.

We said "Thank you" to him and got back into our canoe. He stood on the bank, looking after us till we went around the bend, and for some reason or other I couldn't get him out of my mind for a long time. I haven't got him out yet. He was a nice man, and he was lonesome for boys. It was too bad he didn't have any of his own.

We kept paddling along, with our eyes open sharp. It was worth while to keep your eyes open on the river because there was so much to see—birds, and thousands of turtles sleeping on stones and logs, and sometimes a muskrat. Besides, there were fish jumping every little while, and sounds back among the trees and underbrush that were made by little animals you looked for but couldn't see most of the while. We did see a few squirrels, and once a little bit of a chipmunk. He just sat up on his haunches and looked at us, not scairt a bit till I yelled "Boo!" at him. Then you should have seen him flick away. My, but he was quick! One second he was there and the next he was gone.

I saw Mark take out his watch and look at it, and knew what it meant, all right. He was just seeing if his stomach told the truth about its being dinner-time.

"Well?" says I.

He twisted his big round head on his fat neck and grinned.

"N-not for a half an hour," says he.

"I don't remember saying another word. I was too hungry to do anything but think about eating, and I'll bet Mark was hungrier than I was. When you're nearly starved you don't want to talk, you just want to eat, and every minute between you and food seems like it stretched from noon till midnight.

"Well, sir, I guess being so hungry made us a little careless. We were just coming to a sharp bend, and for the first time we forgot to slow up and look ahead. We just pelted along as though there wasn't a thing in the world to be afraid of. I was looking off to the left when I heard Mark give a startled grunt and saw him dig his paddle into the water and push the nose of the canoe toward shore. I looked. There, up to their waists in the river, were Jiggins and Collins, working over their flatboat that had struck something and tipped over. I dug my paddle in, too.

"It was lucky for us they were busy and had their backs our way, for we weren't more than fifty feet from them. The splash and rush of the current kept the sound of our paddles from them, and we managed to get to shore and hide just on our side of the point. We didn't pull the canoe up; we lifted it. Lifting was quieter. Then we sat down, *plump*! It took the wind right out of our sails."

"Whew," I says, "but that was a narrow one!"

He just shook his head and panted. "It was hot, and we moved pretty sudden, I can tell you."

"We're all r-r-right here," says he, "if we keep quiet and they don't go p-p-prowlin' around. They think we're below them."

"I'd feel more comfortable farther away," I says; but I could see it wouldn't be safe to move. "Wonder how they're gittin' along?"

We craned our necks to see, but it wasn't any use. There was a hummock in the way, and considerable high grass and bushes.

"And we can't eat," I says. "We dassent make a fire."

That was the worst of it.

Mark crawled down to the canoe, though, and came back with a loaf of bread and some butter. The butter was soft and squashy, but we didn't object to that. We wouldn't have objected to anything we could chew and swallow. A meal of bread and butter don't sound like you'd be very interested in it, but, all the same, you'd be mistaken if you thought we weren't. We *enjoyed* it. Between us we ate that whole loaf and looked around for crumbs.

I said before that a fellow is braver when his stomach's full than when he's had to tighten his belt. I felt bolder a lot, and more curious to know what Collins and Jiggins were up to.

"I'm goin' to see if I can't git a squint at 'em," says I.

"B-better stay still," says Mark.

"I *got* to try it," I says, and started crawling on my stomach across the point and through the underbrush. I went slow and cautious, and I don't believe a wild Indian could have done a great deal better when it came to making noise. I didn't make *any*. I didn't know I could move so quiet, and it made me sort of proud of myself. I said to myself I'd show the other fellows what a still one I could be in the woods, and did considerable bragging to myself. And then my heart came up into my mouth so sudden I almost bit it.

I poked my head over the hummock, which was maybe twenty-five feet from where I left Mark, and there, not six feet away, were Collins and Jiggins wringing out their clothes. Whew! I just wilted down and tried not to breathe.

But nothing happened, so I screwed up my courage to lift my head again. They were still busy, and they didn't look as though they would be pleasant company. Both of them looked mad enough to bite themselves, and they weren't saying a word. It was funny, and I had all I could do to keep from snickering. My! how I did wish Mark could see them!

There was Jiggins, fat as anything, with sweat trickling down his face and river-water running down his legs. He must have gone in head first, for his hair was wet and plastery, the way a fellow's is when he takes a dive. Collins wasn't fat. He wasn't so awful lean, either, but the general look of discomfort he wore from head to foot was even funnier than Jiggins. They were both turning and twisting their pants, trying to squeeze all the water out of them. I could imagine how cold and clammy and nasty those clothes were going to feel when they put them on again.

Collins looked at Jiggins and scowled, and Jiggins scowled back. Then all of a sudden Collins began to grin and then to laugh, and Jiggins he began to laugh, and both of them simply laid down on the ground and rolled and yelled.

"I wish you could see yourself," Collins says, as soon as he could speak.

"Um," says Jiggins. "See myself? Oh-ho, neighbor, I hain't getting cheated, to speak of. You're some sight yourself." And then he began to sing that silly tune of his, "Tum-diddle-dum-dum. Tee-dee-diddle-dee-dee."

"It's a risky and adventurous life," says Collins.

"That fat boy would have enjoyed this," says Jiggins, with a grin. "He'd have appreciated it. You bet. This gives 'em a good start, eh? Good big start."

"Don't believe they'd hurry much," says Collins. "They didn't know we had a boat. They'll take it easy, and if I know anything about kids they'll see things to stop and look at."

"If anything delays the fat kid," Jiggins says, emphatic, "it'll be eatin'. He'll have to eat."

"You ought to know," says Collins, with a look at the size of Jiggins.

"Wonder how long they're going to keep to the river?" Jiggins says, shaking his head. "Must know where they're going, eh? They acted like it was all planned out."

"All we can do is follow 'em."

"I'd like to meet somebody to inquire of. We've got to keep track of 'em. Maybe somebody'd know where Mr. Hieronymous Alphabet Bell is, too. Then we could take a short cut to him."

"All I can see to do is just keep ahead. Lucky the boat wasn't busted."

They quit talking and put on their soggy clothes. Their boat was pulled up on the shore, and they got in it again and pushed off.

"Good-by, gentlemen," says I to myself, and felt like standing up to wave my hand after them.

When they were out of sight I got up and went back to Mark. He wanted to know what I saw, and I told him. It made him mad to think he'd missed seeing it.

"Anyhow," says I, to comfort him, "we can make a cup of coffee if you want to."

He wanted to.

# CHAPTER XI

We needed a good rest, so we took one. I couldn't get to sleep, but Mark found no trouble about it at all. He can always eat and sleep. We had been up a long time. It seemed days ago we escaped through the tunnel and began the trip down the Père Marquette, but it was that same morning, and now it was just past noon. While Mark slept I sat around until I was tired of doing nothing, and then I got that *Kidnapped* book out of the canoe and read it. That made the time pass pretty quickly.

Mark didn't wake up till nearly three o'clock. As soon as he'd stretched and rubbed his little eyes open we launched our canoe and started again.

I've told you how the Père Marquette River turned and wriggled and twisted. It wasted an awful lot of time getting to Lake Michigan, and went about five times as far as there was any need of. Some of the water was more enterprising, though. It wasn't all satisfied to wander around aimless-like. This ambitious part of the water was always taking short cuts. How can a river shortcut? Easy—just as easy as falling off a log. When the main part of the river would go sweeping off in a big loop the part that was in a hurry would find a low spot and cut right across the base of the loop. It would be just as if you were making a letter "U" with your pencil and, when it was done, drew a line across the opening at the top of it, connecting the two ends. The folks in that country call these short cuts cut-offs.

A cut-off usually is narrow, sometimes not more than six feet wide, and hardly ever more than ten. And how the current in one of them does pelt along! It goes about twice as fast as in the river, and it isn't going slow in the river, you'd better know. We came to one of them about five o'clock that afternoon. Quite a while before we got to it you could hear the water in it rushing and gurgling.

"Somethin' ahead," I says. "Wonder if it's a rapids."

"S-sounds more like pourin' water down a spout," says Mark.

We went slow so as to be on the safe side. We couldn't see anything that looked dangerous or exciting; in fact, we couldn't see anything at all to make the sound. But in a couple of minnits we came opposite a cut in the bank and could see an eddy turning toward it. We edged over. The water was sweeping through just like it was being poured out of a pitcher. It wasn't a fall, but it was a slant. The water was running down-hill, all right.

"Wonder where it goes?" I asked.

"D-dun'no'," says Mark. "Looks like it might be f-f-fun. Let's slide down it."

That was our first acquaintance with cut-offs.

We turned in the canoe, and all of a sudden the water grabbed it and shot it ahead. We weren't expecting it, and before we knew it we were twisted almost around and nearly banged against the bank. We dug our paddles in, though, and straightened her up. After that all we had to do was hold her straight—the current did the rest. It was like coasting.

Don't think we weren't kept busy, though. There were twists and turns and points and stones and brush-piles. All of these kept getting in the way, and it wasn't so easy as you may think to keep away from them.

After we'd been shooting along for half an hour we whirled around a bend, and there the stream split in two. I looked one way, and there, across the water, lay a big tree that had fallen. As quick as I could I swung the other way, and, *kers-mash*! we crashed against a sharp snag. You could hear it rip the side of the canoe. We hung there a minnit and then swung toward shore, where the current got a good push at the canoe and came pretty near to upsetting it. I jumped out in the water, which was only above my knees, and hung on. Mark jumped, too, but he hit a deeper spot and got in pretty nearly to his shoulders. It was a tussle for a little while, but at last we got the canoe swung around so she was all right, except for the hole in her side. Then we waded ashore.

The place where we landed was on a sharp point where the cut-off divided. The stream pelted down on either side of us, and disappeared in the woods. The ground we stood on was black, oozy marsh. As soon as you picked up a foot your track filled with water.

"N-nice pickle," says Mark.

"Fine," says I.

"Haul her ashore," says he; and we got a grip on the canoe and dragged it up beside us.

"L-lucky I brought that p-paint and canvas," says he, all puffed up about him-self. Mark liked to have folks appreciate what he did, I can tell you.

"Been luckier," I says, "if we hadn't come foolin' down this offshoot. We'd 'a' done better to stick to the river."

"No use f-fussin' about it now. We're here!"

That was just like Mark, too. He never worried about what *might* have hap-pened, but always got to work fixing up what *had* happened.

We took everything out of the canoe and turned the canoe bottom side up. From there on I wasn't much good. Mark was the fellow that fixed it. He pounded and whittled and fussed around till it began to get dark.

"Wish we'd b-brought a lantern," says he.

"So do I," says I. "I hain't in love with campin' out here with no light."

"I mean to f-f-fix the canoe."

"Can't finish it to-night now," I says. "Better leave it and come look for a place to camp. It don't look to me as if there was anything but swamp for miles."

"We'll have to m-m-make a place to camp," says he.

"How?" I asked him. "Up in a tree?"

"We might do that," says he, "if it was n-necessary, but it ain't."

"What, then?"

"I dun'no' yet. Lemme think."

He leaned up against a big tree and began tugging at his puffy cheek. He always does that when he's studying. If he runs onto something harder than usual he whittles. You can make up your mind, when you see him whittling, that pretty soon you'll hear an idea that's an idea. This time he didn't seem to think it was necessary to whittle.

I thought of a bed Mark made once before by cutting four forked stakes and laying poles across them, and then cross-pieces, but here the ground was so soggy and oozy we would have had to drive telegraph-poles to get deep enough to hold. If we made stake-beds they'd be sunk down so we laid in the mud in half an hour.

All the time we were smacking mosquitoes. As soon as we came ashore it looked as if they came swarming down to chase us away. If there had been any way for us to go they would have done it, too. We didn't want to stay. I can't think of any place we wouldn't rather have been.

"I g-g-got it," says Mark at last. "Come on b-b-back where the trees are thicker."

We wallowed back into the woods, feet wet, sweat running off from us in streams, and mosquito-bites from head to foot. I never imagined anybody could be so uncomfortable.

Mark had the ax. After a while he stopped and began measuring between trees. I looked to see if I could study out his scheme, but I couldn't. There were four trees standing in a sort of square about ten feet apart. I could see how we could use them for the posts of a bed if they were cut down, but we didn't have any nails to fasten poles to them, or any other way of doing it that I could see.

Mark measured carefully between two of the trees and then went to cut down a small tree about six inches thick. I helped at that. We carried it back to the four big trees and put it down. Then Mark picked up the ax and began chopping into one of the big trees about three feet from the ground.

"It'll take all night to chop that tree down," I says.

He didn't answer anything, but kept right on chopping. Pretty soon he had a notch cut out about three inches deep. The bottom edge of the notch was parallel with the ground. When he had that finished he chopped another notch in the opposite tree.

"There," says he, "that's a b-b-beginning."

I didn't say anything, because I couldn't guess what he was up to, and it isn't safe to make fun of one of his schemes till you're pretty sure it isn't going to work.

The next thing he did was to cut a chunk off the little tree just long enough to reach from the inside edge of the notch in one tree to the inside edge of the notch in the other. It was a tight fit, and he had to pound to make it go in. But it did go. There, about three feet above the ground, was a six-inch-thick log running from one tree to the other, and up good and solid.

"S-see now?" Mark asked.

I did see. He gave me the ax, and I cut notches in the other two trees, and in them we fitted another small log. The rest was easy. Between the two we laid a lot of poles, and on top of the poles we piled boughs and leaves until we had a good, soft bed. When that was done we had a place to sleep, but we didn't have anything to keep away the mosquitoes. Neither had we had anything to eat.

We built two fires, one to cook by and the other for a smudge. I suppose we could have eaten raw potatoes if we had to, but we didn't have to. Mark fussed around under some bundles and pulled out some bacon he'd sliced at the house, and some potatoes. Then out of a box of sand he dug four eggs. I knew I might have trusted him to see we wouldn't starve.

By the time we had supper cooked and eaten and the things washed up we were plenty tired. We'd have gone off to bed, only we didn't think the mosquitoes would let us sleep.

We sat up awhile in the smudge, but finally I couldn't stand it any longer. It was too nasty on the ground. We both climbed up on the bed and rolled up in our blankets.

"H-hope we find your uncle Hieronymous before another n-night," says Mark.

There's only one good thing I can say about that night—we weren't cold. Everything else in the world was the matter with it. If there hadn't been anything but just the idea of sleeping off there alone in the heart of the woods it would have been very comfortable. How did we know what sort of animal might come along? And there might be snakes! It's easy for Tallow and Plunk to say they wouldn't been nervous, but they were back in uncle's house, where they could lock the door and get in bed. You don't want to say you would be so mighty brave in a place until you've been in it.

We did sleep some. Most likely we slept more than we thought we did. At any rate, it wasn't enough. I was waked up just about the crack of day, and I was mean enough to wake Mark up for company. We laid and talked a spell, and then got up to finish fixing the canoe and have our breakfast.

It didn't take so very long to patch up the canoe so it would float and didn't leak. Breakfast was pretty thin, too. We didn't feel like cooking, somehow.

The next thing on the program was to haul the canoe around the fallen tree and get into it. This wasn't so easy as it sounds, especially the getting-into-it part. We tugged and pulled her over to the water, but the bank dropped off sharp, and the current just more than rushed by. Mark tied a rope to the canoe and got in. She was half in the water then. I pushed her along till she was all afloat, but I didn't dare let go my hold on the rope to jump in myself. I stood three or four feet from the shore, pulling for dear life to keep the canoe from getting away from me.

"P-p-put the rope around that tree," says Mark, pointing. "Then th-throw the end to me. I can hold her that way, and let her g-go when I want to."

I did what he said and got the end of the rope to him, all right. It was as simple as could be. I could have thought of it myself, only somehow I didn't happen to. Mark was one of the kind of fellows that usually happen to think of what they need to think of.

I scrambled aboard, and Mark let go the rope. We spun around twice before we could get control of the canoe again, but no harm came of it.

The stream carried us along at a ripping speed. We began to breathe in the good air, and after a while the tiredness was breathed out of us and we began to enjoy ourselves. It was pretty in those woods. All along the edge of the stream were flowers, and birds were flying overhead, and turtles and frogs were splashing in as we went by. Somehow it didn't seem as if a human being ever saw it all before. There wasn't a thing to make you think a man ever was near. It was just woods, woods, woods, and stream, stream, stream. I'll bet it didn't look a bit different when Columbus discovered America.

As I say, we were enjoying ourselves and forgetting all about how bad a night we passed. We were looking forward to meeting Uncle Hieronymous pretty soon and warning him so he wouldn't lose his mine, and then, we said, we could drive back to the house and take things easy the rest of the summer.

We planned all sorts of things we would do. Mark just got through plannin' how we would go over to the lake and explore all around it when we spun around the last bend of the cut-off and shot out into the main river. That was sort of a relief, but it wasn't any relief when somebody not a hundred feet up-stream from us yelled, *"There they are!"*

We looked quick, and who should we see but Collins and Jiggins, in their boat, coming for us as hard as they could come.

# CHAPTER XII

Maybe you've never noticed it, but when anything dangerous or exciting or unexpected happens your body does something or other without your knowing what it is going to do and without your asking it to do it. You say you were startled into doing whatever it was. Maybe that's the explanation of it, but Mark Tidd says it's the instinct of self-preservation. He knows a lot of words like that.

Well, this instinct of self-preservation made Mark and me do the same thing at the same time. It made us dig our paddles into the water and scoot down-stream as fast as we could make the canoe go.

A canoe is a lot faster and easier to handle than a scow—even a special scow made for the river. When we first saw Jiggins and Collins in their boat they weren't more than a hundred feet from us, and they had the advantage of getting started first. After we got started they didn't gain, though. We didn't gain much, either, because what our canoe gave us in lightness they made up in strength.

They were too busy to yell at us, and we had our hands full without doing any talking in particular. We just dug in.

After a few minutes Mark whispered, "How we m-makin' it?"

"Holdin' our own," says I.

At that rate they'd catch us, or at least Mark said so.

"We'll t-tire first," says he. "They can k-keep it up longer than we can."

"We might's well give up, then," says I, "and save ourselves all this work."

"Can you p-p-paddle a little harder?" he asked.

"Not much," says I.

"For as long as you can," says he, "p-paddle as hard as you can. See if we can't g-gain a little."

It seemed like my back would break and my arms come out by the roots, but I worked just a little harder, and so did Mark. I looked back and it did seem as if we were some farther away from the other boat than we were.

"Keep it up," says I.

We did, and we gained. At last we gained so much we turned a bend out of their sight. This didn't mean we were far away. I should say it didn't. It couldn't have been two hundred feet at the very most. The turn was sharp, and like a letter "S." The part we turned into was like the lower loop of the letter, and right at the narrowest point were some tall weeds and bushes that grew right down to the shore.

"L-looks as if there was a stream went in t-there," Mark stuttered.

We didn't have time to plan or figure. Mark was the sort to go slow and plan and plot when there was time for it, but when he had to decide quick he could do it, and quicker than anybody else I ever knew.

"T-try it," he snapped, and swung the canoe toward the weeds.

I helped. It was about the only chance we had to fool Jiggins and Collins, and it wasn't such a very good one, either. If there was water through those bushes, all right. Maybe they wouldn't see we'd gone in that way. If there wasn't water our goose was cooked, and no mistake about it.

But there was water. The bushes almost stopped us—almost. We pushed our paddles against the bottom and shoved our way through. Quick as a wink Mark turned the canoe again, for there was a sort of pond back there that gave a little room. He sent us splashing over to one side so we were out of sight of the opening we came through. After that there was nothing to do but wait.

We didn't have to wait very long. In about a minnit we heard the other boat come floundering along. I thought it was going by, all right, and that we wouldn't be discovered. Mark's face looked disappointed, actually disappointed. But the boat stopped. Then its blunt end came nosing through the high grasses and bushes, and Jiggins's round face came into sight. Mark sighed, and it really was a sigh of relief.

"I d-d-didn't think we'd fool 'em this way," he said. "I'd 'a' been disappointed in Jiggins if we had."

That was it. Mark had made up his mind Jiggins was a great man just because both of them were fat and looked something alike; and he would have been disappointed if Jiggins had been easy to bamboozle. I expect he had it all planned out he'd get a lot more credit for getting the best of a sharp man than of one that didn't have many brains.

Jiggins saw us, and his eyes twinkled. "Hello, boys!" says he. "Glad to see you. Most p'ticularly glad to see you. You wouldn't believe it, but we've been *looking* for you. Collins and myself, we've actually been trying to find you."

Mark sort of grinned. "I didn't f-f-figger on that boat," says he, pointing to the scow Jiggins was in.

"You should always figure on everything. Better luck next time. Can't always win."

Collins stood up and looked over at us. "Quite considerable of a race for a few minnits," he says. "For boys that don't know much about paddling you're pretty good paddlers."

I will say they were good-natured men and pleasant company. If they hadn't been the enemy we'd have liked them fine. I'm not sure we didn't like them pretty average well as it was. It never occurred to us to be afraid of them; we knew they wouldn't hurt us, whatever happened. All they would do was try to get to Uncle Hieronymous before we could and to keep us from giving them away. Somehow it seemed more like a game where you had to use your brains than an adventure out in the woods.

"Come on out," says Jiggins. "Be sociable."

There wasn't anything else to do but come, so we pushed the canoe over to the flatboat.

"Now," says Jiggins, "I think I'll be easier in my mind if we divide up a bit, eh? Fat man and fat boy in this boat; thin man and thin boy in that boat. More appropriate." While we were making the change he leaned back and sang, "Tee-deedle-dee-deedle-dum-deedle-dee," over and over again.

Mark and Jiggins started out first, and Collins and I followed. When we got out on the river we kept as clost together as we could so we could talk. But mostly we couldn't keep side by side, for the channel was too narrow and winding. Even when the river was wide enough for two boats abreast, which it usually was, there were sand-bars and shallows and snags and dead-heads. Why, we almost needed a pilot to get along at all!

Collins and I had a pretty good time. He knew lots of interesting things about the woods and animals and camping and hunting. Mark and Jiggins seemed to be enjoying themselves, too, for they kept talking to each other as solemn as owls. Usually when Mark has that awful solemn look he's making some sort of a joke, and I persume Jiggins is the same way. Neither of them laughed out loud or let on there was anything funny, but I bet anybody else would have laughed till he split at what they were saying to each other.

After a while we drew up alongside for a little while.

Jiggins turned to me and says, "Uncle Hieronymous down this way?"

Maybe he was expecting to take me by surprise and get something out of me, but he didn't. I just grinned at him and Mark and told him uncle was one of the hardest men to locate exactly I ever saw.

"Well," says Jiggins, "if he's along the river we'll see him, won't we? And if he isn't you won't see him. Very good. No harm done either way. We'll find him some day. No fear. Can't miss."

"Yes," says Mark, "we'll sh-sh-show him to you some day."

"When?" asked Jiggins, grinning a little.

"Any time after we've had a f-f-few minutes' talk with him."

"Do you know where he is?" Collins put in.

Mark looked at him a minute before he decided what to say. Then he says, "Honest to g-g-goodness, Mr. Collins, we don't know exactly."

"I see we'll have to keep you right with us," says Collins.

"And I'm glad of it," says Jiggins. "Good company, eh? Surely. Enjoy ourselves. Never quarrel. You try to win; we try to win—no hard feelings."

"That's all right," I says, "but do you think it's very honest to try to get away Uncle Hieronymous's mine?"

"Honest? Why not?" You could see he was really surprised. He couldn't see why it wasn't all right to buy a man's land for a little bit of money when really it was worth a whole lot because there was a mine on it the owner didn't know about. "D'you think I ought to tell him about the mine?" says he. "That's bosh," he says. "'Twouldn't be business. If your uncle wants to know if there's a mine on his land let him look for it. We had to."

I suppose there was something to his side of it. He and Collins, or whoever it was they worked for, had found the mine, and it did look as if they ought to have something out of it. Uncle never would have found it. I tell you it's pretty hard to judge other folks and say when they're honest or dishonest. Mark says it depends a lot on the way you look at things or how you've been brought up. As for me, honest is honest and dishonest is dishonest, and I can't quite get it into my head how anything makes it different. Maybe it does, though. At any rate, I couldn't get to feeling Jiggins and Collins were *bad*.

We just dawdled along that day. When we stopped for dinner we took two or three hours to it and didn't start out again till the hottest part of the afternoon was over.

Jiggins was a good cook. He and Mark 'tended to getting the meal, but this was one of the times Mark didn't do much but look on. Jiggins showed him things. You could see, without half looking, that Mark thought a heap of the fat man. Mark right down admired him.

After dinner Mark and I sat down together and talked a spell.

"He's a g-g-great man," says Mark.

"Shucks!" says I.

"He's beat us so f-far, hain't he?"

"'Twasn't nothin' but luck. Are you 'fraid they're goin' to beat us all the way through?"

I knew Mark Tidd never would admit any such thing as that. Not him! "'Course n-not," says he. "But it's goin' t-to be p-p-perty hard sleddin' for us. If it was just Collins I wouldn't worry a speck. But Jiggins! He's g-g-got a head for thinkin', he has."

"Got any scheme for escapin'?" I asked him.

"Not yet. I'm p-p-plannin', though. It's got to be at night. If I've f-f-figgered right we got to-night and to-morrow night. 'Tain't l-likely we'll come up with your uncle till day after to-morrow, g-g-goin' at the rate we are."

"Never put off till to-morrer night what you kin do to-night," I says.

"I wish I knew m-m-more about the country," he stuttered. "Then we c-could leave the river and cut across lots. As it is we got to st-st-stick to the water."

"Well," I says, "you do the plannin' and tell me when you're ready to do somethin'. I'm goin' to take a nap."

The last I remember seeing of him he was leaning back against a tree, with his little eyes shut, and he was pinching and tugging away at his fat cheek like all-git-out. He was thinking. Next thing he'd do would be get out his jack-knife and whittle. When he did that—*look out!*

Collins waked me up, and he and I got into the canoe. Mark and Jiggins followed close behind us in the flatboat, and I could hear Jiggins singing away at his foolish tune, "Tum-deedle-dee-deedle-dum," and so on, without any finish at all.

We camped that night on a sandy flat. While Jiggins and Mark got supper Collins and I fixed things up for the night. We cut a lot of boughs and twigs for our beds and pulled up the canoe and the flatboat and turned them over the supplies, so if it rained nothing would be spoiled. Then we stretched a clothes-line between two trees and threw over it a big piece of grimy canvas that Jiggins and Collins had brought along. The edges of this we pulled out and staked down so we had a pretty fair shelter. Of course, it was open at the ends, but it would keep off the dew and the rain if there wasn't much wind. Mark came and looked at it.

"B-better dig a ditch around it," says he.

"What for?" Collins asked.

"If it rains," says Mark, "the d-d-ditch'll carry off the water that runs off the t-tent. If you don't have a d-d-ditch you'll have a p-p-puddle right where you sleep."

Collins allowed that sounded sensible, so we scooped out a little trench all the way around, with a canal leading away toward the river. By that time supper was ready.

When we were through eating we built up the fire so it would give light and keep us warm. Jiggins and Collins walked around to get the stiffness out of their legs and to smoke. Mark and I sat down, or, rather, laid down, close to the fire.

"I g-g-got a scheme," says Mark.

"What is it?" I asked.

Just then Collins strolled over our way, and Mark shut up tight as a locked door. I looked around for Jiggins, but I couldn't see him. I supposed he'd just walked off to look around a bit, but that wasn't it. Maybe if I'd called it to Mark's attention things would have turned out differently from what they did, but I didn't think it was important. You never can tell, though. After this I'm not going to overlook anything, no matter how silly I may think it is. Mark says the silliest things on the surface are sometimes the deepest down underneath. This was one of them. Mark said Jiggins was a great man, and—well, I came pretty close to agreeing with him before morning.

# CHAPTER XIII

So you can understand just what happened that night I will tell you as careful-ly as I can just how our camp lay and where everything in and around it was. Then you'll be able to see how hard it was to plan a way for Mark and me to escape, and what a lot of brains Mark Tidd had to have to figure out ahead of time just about what Jiggins and Collins would do with us. I never could have done it. If I was going to think up a scheme to get away I'd have to wait till we were all fixed the way we were going to be. Maybe then I could have figgered something out; but with Mark it was different. He looked ahead. He was always putting himself into somebody else's shoes and trying to think just the way they would think. I couldn't do that. But Mark would just make believe he was the other fellow, and you'd be surprised to see how many times he hit it right.

Well, the camp was on a sandy flat shaped like a triangle. The river ran past the base of it, and high banks climbed almost straight up from the two sides. The whole thing was covered with trees and shrubs and grasses, except back about the middle, where there was a small bare patch of sand, and here we had our tent. The base of the triangle was about two hundred feet long, and each of the sides was a little more than that, I should say.

When we came we hauled up our boats at the up-stream end of the flat and turned them over there. That spot was over a hundred feet from the camp, and you couldn't see the boats from the tent. The fire was at the end of the tent that pointed up-stream. The supplies and paddles and oars were all left under the boats.

When we turned in Collins slept across one opening of the tent and Jiggins across the other. Their feet touched canvas on one side and their heads touched it on the other. Mark and I slept between. We were so close together, when we all got in, that we touched, and before a fellow could roll over he came pretty close to having to ask the man next him to help. Add to that that Collins and Jiggins both bragged about how lightly they slept and said the least noise or touch would wake them, and you'll see they had us pretty average safe. We couldn't wiggle without waking one of them.

Before we went to bed we sat by the fire quite a while and talked. Mark got to talking about lassoes and bragged considerable about how he could throw one of them. Jiggins made fun of him, and Mark said get a rope for him and he'd show what he could do. It was pretty dark then, but Collins fished a piece of line about forty feet long out of the mess of stuff under the boats and told Mark to go ahead.

Mark made a noose in the rope and had me run back and forth in the firelight while he whirled the thing around his head and threw at me. He *was* pretty good at it, and no mistake. He could catch me every time, and about the way he wanted to. First he'd get me around the neck, and then by one foot, and sometimes by a hand if it happened to be sticking out. He told me afterward he'd been practising it in his back yard ever since a Wild West show came to our country-seat. He'd kept still about it because he wanted to give Plunk and Tallow and me a surprise when he got so he could throw good.

We fussed around like that for half an hour, and then Mark said he was tired. He tossed the rope off to the side of the tent where there was a sapling growing about fifteen feet away.

"Better get some more firewood," says Collins, and he and Jiggins and I went off looking for dry sticks. Mark didn't go far, though. While we were busy he tied his rope tight to the tree and carried one end up and pushed it under the tent. There was about twenty feet to spare, so he cut that off and brought it inside.

Of course, I didn't know that till afterward, but he told me just how he did it. The piece of rope he cut off he laid through the tent from one end to the other about a foot from the side where our feet would go. So nobody'd notice it he pushed it down under the boughs we had to sleep on. Then he went back and got an armful of sticks and threw them down by the fire. When we got back with our loads he lay there with his eyes shut, looking as sleepy as an old frog. He yawned and yawned and rubbed his eyes and said he guessed he'd go to bed. I went in with him.

We got fixed before Collins and Jiggins were through their smoke.

"Move around c-c-consid'able," says Mark in a whisper. "Sort of git them used to h-h-havin' you rub against them."

I couldn't see any sense to that, but, all the same, I said I'd do it. You can't see any sense to lots of things Mark wants you to do, but usually you find out he knew what he was talking about.

"K-k-keep awake if you can," he says next, stuttering like anything. "I'll p-pinch you every little while, and you p-pinch me. That'll do it, I guess."

Then Jiggins and Collins came in. Collins laid down next to me, and Jiggins took the other end. They said good night as polite as if we were back home instead of out in the woods, or as if they were visitors instead of guards. Mark and I said good night back again, and then everybody kept quiet for a spell. I got drowsy.

The next thing that happened was Jiggins speaking.

"For goodness' sake, son," says he to Mark, "keep still. Be quiet. You roll like a boat in a heavy sea. Go to sleep."

Mark quieted down a little, and I remembered to stir about like he said. Collins stood it a few minnits and then nudged me with his elbow. "Binney," says he, "want me to sing you to sleep?"

"No," says I. "Why?"

"Because," says he, "I'd be willing to do 'most anything to get you still. You wiggle like an angleworm."

"I hain't comfortable," I told him.

"Well," says he, "I hope you tire yourself out pretty soon. You're tirin' me."

At that Mark pinched my arm.

We kept quiet after that for quite a while, maybe half an hour. Every minnit or so Mark would pinch me, and if he missed I'd pinch him. That way there wasn't any danger of our going to sleep.

Both Collins and Jiggins began to snore. I laid as still as I could and never wiggled even an eyelash. After a while Mark nudged me with his elbow.

"S-s-squirm some," says he, under his breath.

I moved my legs and twisted my shoulders. Collins sort of grunted in his sleep and threw up his arm, but he didn't wake. I could feel Mark moving on the other side of me, and then Jiggins muttered something in a drowsy voice. He didn't sound a quarter awake.

There was another wait, then Mark whispered in my ear to snuggle as close to Collins as I could so as to give him room. I did. He moved over so part of him was on top of me, and that left him clear of Jiggins. There was the dimmest sort of light from the coals in front of the tent, so I could just make out Mark and guess at what he was doing. The first thing he did was to get his jack-knife out of his pocket and, cautious as anything, cut a slit about a foot and a half high in the canvas. He reached through that and got hold of the rope. He began to pull. Now you'll see it was a lot easier for him to haul himself out by degrees like he was a cork in a bottle than it would be for him to move around and get up and step over Jiggins. That would have made a commotion and considerable noise, while by pulling himself out a couple of inches at a time you could hardly notice anything at all was happening. If I hadn't been awake and looking and listening I never would have discovered what he was at at all.

My heart was beating like somebody was pounding on it with a mallet. It was exciting, I can tell you. The longer it took and the slower and more deliberate Mark was the more exciting it got, until before his feet disappeared through the slit I could have up and hollered.

As soon as I dared I scrooched over in front of the slit in the canvas and grabbed the rope like Mark did. It wasn't any trick at all to inch myself out, and before very long I got up outside and looked around for Mark.

We weren't safe yet by a long ways. No, sir, we were not. Collins and Jiggins were asleep not six feet from us, and the least noise might wake them up. Then there was danger one of them might happen to wake and feel for us. He'd find us gone, and it wouldn't take him long to get after us, you can bet. We didn't stay around there.

One of the funniest sights in the world is to watch Mark Tidd tiptoe. It's sort of like a hippopotamus trying to waltz. But it is surprising how quiet he can go. He's lighter on his feet than I am, and he weighs pretty close to three times as much.

We went straight back away from the tent and then took a wide swing around to the boats.

"Q-quiet now," says Mark. "Shove in the canoe."

We lifted it and set it on the edge of the river and pushed it in.

"I'll hold her," says Mark, "while you g-g-git the p-p-paddles and things." He was so excited he stuttered until he sounded almost like a gasolene-engine that was out of kilter.

I grabbed what came first. Anything that felt like it could be eaten was what I wanted to make sure of. In three minnits I had the boat as full as I dared make it. Then I went back after the paddles.

Well, sir, I looked under and over and between and among for them, but not a paddle was there to be seen. I moved things and rooted into the sand and went around near-by trees to see if they were stood up out of sight, but all I got was a pair of scratched hands.

"Mark," says I, "there hain't no paddles."

"What?" says he, like somebody'd hit him in the stomach.

"The paddles are gone," I said.

He sat plump down on the sand and let his head lop over forward. You could tell by the way he acted he was ashamed. He was cut.

"I m-m-might 'a' known it," says he. "I m-m-might 'a' seen it."

"Shucks!" says I. "Nobody could have guessed it."

"It's exactly what I'd 'a' d-d-done in his place," he says. He sighed, and then: "And I wasn't undervaluin' him, n-n-neither. It was n-n-nothin' but carelessness."

"Pickles!" says I. "Let's make the best of it."

"How?" says he.

"Find a board and use it for a paddle," says I.

He looked at me disgusted and shook his head. "I'm s'prised at you, B-B-Binney. You don't think Jiggins 'u'd 'a' l-left any b-boards around handy, do you? Not him."

"Well," I says next, "what's the matter with just piling into the canoe and shovin' off? We'd git somewheres, and somewheres else is better 'n bein' here."

He thought a minnit or so. "'Tain't p-p-practical," says he. "We dun'no' where we are, do we? Nor how to g-git any place? But," says he, "there hain't n-n-nothin' else *to* do. We'll run ashore or git wrecked or somethin', but come on."

I held the boat while he scrambled in, and was just going to get in myself when Jiggins spoke up from the dark behind us and says: "Better not start off in the dark, boys. Better not. 'Tain't advisable. See it for yourselves. Stay ashore. To be sure."

I was so surprised I didn't say a word, and I guess Mark was surprised too. But he didn't let on.

"I was expectin' you'd c-c-come along next," says he.

"I sort of figgered you'd try something to-night," says Jiggins.

"It was carelessness, me f-f-forgettin' those paddles," says Mark.

"Fellow can't think of everything," says Jiggins, like he was trying to keep Mark from feeling bad. "Better come back to bed. Need sleep. So do I. So does Collins."

Mark got out of the canoe, slow as molasses. He didn't like to come a bit, but he couldn't help himself.

"N-n-next time," says he, "I won't forget anythin'."

"When'll next time be?" Jiggins asked, with a sort of chuckle.

"It won't be to-night," says Mark.

"There hain't much time left," I whispered to him.

"There's t-to-morrow and t-to-morrow night," he says.

"Somehow I don't feel a bit sleepy," I told Mark.

"N-n-neither do I." He stopped a minnit and tugged at his button of a nose. "But I'm hungry. L-let's get somethin' to eat."

We rummaged around till we found a box of crackers, and we started in on them.

"Hey!" says Collins, from the tent. "What you up to now?"

"Eatin'," says Mark.

We heard somebody stirring around, and then Jiggins crawled out.

"What you got?" he asked. "Um. Lemme see. Crackers, eh? Gimme some. Gimme a handful. What you mean, eating without offering me any? Always willing to eat. Always."

We passed the box to him, and he took half a dozen. You couldn't get away from it, he was a lot like Mark Tidd. Fat, always hungry, and had a lot of brains. I wondered if Mark would be like him when he grew up, but I thought not. I don't know why, but there was something different about Mark. It was hard to figure out just what it was, but I guess it was a combination of things. Mark was funnier and liked funny things more. And he was surer of himself. When Mark started to do a thing he never had the least bit of doubt he'd come out all right. Jiggins, it seemed to me, was a little worried at times.

"Got enough?" Collins called. "'Cause I want to get to sleep."

"That's why he's thin," says Jiggins to Mark. "No interest in food. Always sticking up his nose at eating. Thin. Skinny. Don't weigh any more'n a good-sized feather. It's his stomach. Worries about it. Didn't eat between meals. Silly, eh? We don't think that way, eh, son?"

"No," says Mark, with a grin.

It was peculiar how good-natured everybody was. Of course, Jiggins and Collins had a right to be because they'd come out ahead; but Mark and I didn't hold it up against them. Funny, isn't it? We chatted as pleasant as if we were close friends instead of genuine enemies and opponents-like. Most folks would have growled and sulked and scowled at each other, but not one of us did. If I've got to have enemies that's the way I'd like to have them.

We turned in pretty quick, and I didn't know another thing till Collins woke me up in the morning by pouring a cup of water on me. He was laughing like he thought it was funny. So were Jiggins and Mark. Everybody seems to see how comical a thing like that is except the fellow the water falls on.

# CHAPTER XIV

The third of our days on the river wasn't what you could call exciting. It started out hot and got hotter. It wasn't so bad for Collins and me, but Mark Tidd and Jiggins *fried*. We kept on, though. Jiggins said he was tired of being where he couldn't get a square meal, and, heat or no heat, he was going to get where there was food in large quantities.

We traveled the same way we did the day before—that is, Mark and Jiggins in the boat and Collins and me in the canoe. Along toward the middle of the morning we saw a farm-house back about a quarter of a mile from the river. Jiggins pointed.

"Milk," says he. "Home-made bread. Um. Pickles. Did you hear that? *Pickles.* Seems like I couldn't get along without a pickle. A long pickle. Maybe sweet, maybe sour—I don't care."

Mark looked excited. "Pie," says he. "I bet they got p-p-pie. Cherry-pie! L-l-let's stop."

Collins looked at me and grinned, and I looked at Collins and grinned. It was funny the way both those fat folks did let their minds run to eating. Not that I would have thrown a piece of pie into the river if somebody had offered it to me, and Collins wasn't the sort of fellow to use a glass of fresh milk to wash his face with, but it was more—what d'you call it?—incidental-like with us. With them it was about the most important thing there was. I'd like to enjoy something the way Mark Tidd enjoys eating. I've heard it makes you dull to eat a lot, but it didn't work that way with Mark. He always could think better after he'd eaten a meal big enough to keep a family two days.

Of course, we went ashore. There would have been a rebellion right there if we hadn't. We walked back through the low ground and found a lane running up to the house. It led to the barn-yard and around a low shed where the farmer kept his wagon. Where it went we went. We straggled around the corner of that shed into the yard, and then we stopped. We stopped sudden and short, and everybody said something startled, for there, coming toward us like he meant business and a good deal of it, was the biggest white bulldog I ever saw. Maybe he looked bigger than he was, but, allowing for that, he was plenty big.

I don't know what the rest did. Right there Binney Jenks was a pretty busy kid with no time to fool with anybody. I turned and went up the fence and scrambled on top of that shed so quick it must have looked like I did it in one jump. Collins was about a tenth of a second behind me. Mark and Jiggins, being so fat, weren't quite as quick, but they did considerable moving when you take everything into consideration. Both of them were on the fence and the dog was jumping at their feet. Mark got on the shed next, and that left nobody but Jiggins in reach. I never saw a dog put his mind to getting a man the way that bulldog did. He acted like it was necessary for him to have a chunk of Jiggins, and it looked, too, as though he was going to come pretty close to getting what he was after.

Collins and I sat still. We were sort of startled out of our wits, I guess, but not Mark. He was busy the minnit he got on the roof. By luck there was a long pole up there—about twenty feet long, I guess; Mark grabbed it and crouched at the very edge of the roof. Then Mister Dog jumped for Jiggins. Maybe you don't think he was a surprised animal! Just as he jumped Mark poked, and he poked good and hard. The pole took the dog in the ribs, and you could hear him say, "Urgh," or something like that. He went kerflop and head over heels.

"H-h-hurry up!" says Mark to Jiggins.

Jiggins hurried.

The dog wasn't through, though. He took two more licks at Jiggins before the fat man could clamber onto the shed, and then sat down and scowled at us. If he couldn't get us he was going to see we didn't get away.

It was sort of funny. I looked over at Mark and says, "How d'you like the pie?"

He grinned. "Guess they p-put p-p-pepper in it by mistake," says he.

"Doesn't look as if anybody was home," says Collins, who had been looking at the house.

We all looked then, and, sure enough, the house was all closed up. Most likely everybody had gone to town and left the dog to look after things. They picked the right one to leave, all right. There wasn't anybody who could have done better.

Well, there we were, four of us on a roof, with the sun beating down like sixty, with nothing to drink and nothing to eat, and no chance that we could see of getting down before the folks who lived there got home. That's what comes of thinking about your stomach all the time. If appetites hadn't been invented we never would have met that dog, and he was an acquaintance I would have been perfectly willing not to have known.

Ten minnits before that Jiggins and Collins were our enemies. If ever you have one you want to make an ally of, I recommend a bulldog and the hot top of a shed. We were partners in a second. We might be enemies again after we got down, but while we were there we were one tight combination. All we thought was bulldog, and what to say to him to persuade him we weren't meant for food. He was stubborn, though. It didn't matter what we said or how kindly we spoke to him or argued with him, he wouldn't change his mind. If we couldn't be inside him he had it figgered out we were in the next best place, and he'd keep us there. He was unreasonable about it.

"Let's holler," I says.

"N-no use," says Mark. "Nobody to hear you. There hain't another house in sight."

"Wish we had a gun," says Collins, with one eye on the bulldog.

"Wouldn't shoot him if we had," says Jiggins. "Certainly not. No fault of his. Doing his duty. Good dog. Like to own him. Our fault, eh? We came in his yard. Who asked us? Nobody did. Well?"

Come to think of it, we didn't have much right to complain about that dog. He was doing what his master told him to do, and he was making a good job of it.

"We've got to do something," says Collins, with sweat trickling down his nose. "We can't stay here all day."

"L-l-looks like we couldn't do anything else," says Mark. And Jiggins grinned.

"There must be some way of coaxin' doggie to let us down," I says.

"Oh," says Collins, "he'll let us down, all right. The trouble is, what will he do when we've got down?"

Mark sat down and pulled his hat over his eyes. He had his cheek between his thumb and finger and was pinching it so it looked white.

"Thinkin'," says I to Collins. "He'll git us down. You see."

Collins just grinned sort of sickly. He didn't seem to have any great confidence in Mark, but then he didn't know Mark as well as I did.

After a few minnits Mark got up and walked to the edge of the shed away from the dog. He stood there measuring with his eye how far it was to a sort of lean-to against the side of the barn. I went over and looked, too. It must have been twelve or fifteen feet—too far to jump, by considerable.

"Great if we had a bridge," says I.

"There's m-m-more ways of crossin' a river than on a b-b-bridge," says he.

"Yes," I told him, "you can wade. But the wadin' hain't very healthy right here."

"Hum!" says he, and turned around to where he laid the pole he had used to poke the dog with. "H-how'd that do?" he asked me.

"Nobody could walk across it or even crawl across, and if you were to hang by your hands and go over that way the dog 'u'd get your legs."

"Binney," says Mark, patronizing-like, "what were you and Tallow and Plunk doing in Plunk's back yard all last week?"

I thought back and remembered we'd been pole-vaulting. I said so.

"Well?" says Mark.

All of a sudden it hit me. I felt pretty cheap, too. There I was, the fellow that was interested in pole-vaulting and things like that, and here the first time in my life it really would have come in handy I overlooked it altogether. But my head isn't like Mark's. He stores up in his everything he sees, thinking maybe he can use it some day.

"I kin vault across, I guess," I told him, "but you and Jiggins never could. The pole hain't built that wouldn't bust under you."

"We don't n-need to," says he.

"What's this?" Collins asked. He and Jiggins had been talking on the other side of the roof and hadn't heard what was going on.

"Binney says he can v-vault onto that other shed," says Mark.

"What of it?"

"Can you do it?" Mark asked me.

I didn't like it very well, I'll admit. First, there was the dog to get me if I missed; second, the place I was to land wasn't level, but sloping; and the third, I couldn't get a very good start from the roof we were on. But I couldn't own up I was afraid before folks, so I up and says I'd be tickled to death.

"But what good'll that do?" Collins asked.

"Binney'll get through that l-l-little window into the barn," says Mark. "There's always rope in a barn. He'll get that and throw it over to me. Then I'll l-l-lasso the dog."

"Um," says Jiggins. "Good scheme. Ought to have thought of it myself. But I didn't. Quick, ain't he? Eh? Quicker'n a flash."

"Gimme the pole," says I.

I went to the edge of the roof and looked across. It looked about a mile, now that I had to vault it, and the ground seemed like it was fifty-seven feet away. Also the dog, seeing we were fooling around that edge of the roof, strolled around and was sitting there looking up at me with an expression I didn't like. It wasn't what you could call inviting.

I poked my pole out to the ground in the middle. It reached that far, all right. The only question was whether I had the strength to swing myself all the way across. I saw I'd have to take a run to do it.

Running on that sloping, slippery roof didn't look much like I'd have any luck doing it. But Mark saved the day. I might have known he'd foresee that difficulty.

"T-t-take off your shoes," says he.

Easy, wasn't it? All you have to do is think of it, and there isn't anything to it at all. But somehow nobody thought of it but Mark.

I slipped off my shoes, measured on the pole where I ought to grip it, and went to the far end of the shed. Mark and Jiggins and Collins were looking at me with their faces sort of set and their jaws square. I grinned at them, though I didn't feel much like grinning.

"Here goes," says I, and I ran across that roof as tight as I could let it. My pole landed good and solid right between the two sheds and I swung out and over. I could feel the pole bending under me, and I could hear the dog growl and come for it, but I didn't look down. There wasn't time. That other roof seemed to be shooting out at me, so I just lifted up my feet and went bang down on it. If it hadn't been for the pole I'd have slid off onto the ground, but I held it tight and scrambled to my feet. I was considerable skinned up, but it didn't hurt any, because I felt so good because I'd got across. I was sort of proud of it. Mark was standing right at the edge of the other roof, and you never saw anybody look so relieved. When he spoke his voice was sort of husky and he stuttered like anything.

MY POLE LANDED GOOD AND SOLID RIGHT BETWEEN THE TWO
SHEDS, AND I SWUNG OUT AND OVER

"B-b-b-bully for you, B-Binney," says he, and then stopped sudden. It made me feel good, I can tell you, to have him say that and to know he'd been worried about me. When you know a fellow like Mark Tidd it makes you pretty glad when you're sure he really likes you. And a word of praise from him means a lot, because he don't praise very often.

"Can you open the window?" says Collins, after he and Jiggins had added onto what Mark said about my doing a good job.

I tried. It shoved up easy, and I threw my leg over the sill. "So long," I called to them and ducked inside.

It was the harness-room I landed in, all smelly with leather and grease, and sort of dim so I couldn't see very well to get around. I stood still to let my eyes get used to it, and then looked for a rope. There didn't seem to be any there, so I opened the door and went out into the big room of the barn. Over opposite were the stalls, and in one of them was a horse. It was one of those big, square box-stalls, and that accounts for the horse sticking his nose out toward me and whick-ering. I like horses. Dogs are all right, but for real friendship and usefulness and all-around bullyness give me a horse. If I was a millionaire I'd have as many as Barnum's circus.

I couldn't help going over to speak to this fellow. He whickered again, in-viting-like, and I let the rope go awhile till I could have a little talk with him. He stretched out his nose to me, and I patted it. Then I stopped and craned my neck to look at his legs, for his face seemed mighty familiar. There was a sort of white triangle on his nose, and if he had two white feet that meant he was a horse I was interested in particular. So I craned my neck over like I said before, and, sure enough, there were the white feet.

"Well, Alfred," says I, pretty nearly flabbergasted to see him, "what you doin' here?"

Alfred never said a word, but nuzzled at me and begged for a lump of sugar.

"Alfred," says I, "where's Uncle Hieronymous Alphabet Bell, and when d'you expect him back here?"

Of course, he couldn't tell me, but just his being there was enough to let on Uncle Hieronymous couldn't be many miles away. Uncle wouldn't have left his horse where he couldn't get to see him often. He probably was boarding Alfred here while he worked on the river.

"Well," says I to myself, "what had I better do?"

When you get in a place where you aren't sure what to do next, don't do any-thing. I just stood there and patted Alfred and figgered. The more I figgered the more muddled I got, and I sure did wish Mark Tidd was there to talk it over with. But he wasn't. I had to depend on myself this time.

I thought so long I bet those folks out on the hot top of the shed thought I'd got lost or eaten up, but I wasn't worrying about them just then. I let them do the worrying. Anyhow, two of them were enemies, and that made the unpleasantness two to one. Mark should have been willing to stand that, shouldn't he? Wouldn't you be willing to be uncomfortable if you could see two enemies being just as un-comfortable alongside? Well, maybe you wouldn't. Likely I didn't see it the same way Mark did, for the barn was cool and comfortable. I couldn't make up my mind what I ought to do, so I went hunting for a rope again. I found a good long one and slung it over my shoulder. Then I went back into the harness-room after saying good-by to Alfred, and scrambled through the window onto the roof of the shed.

Mark and Jiggins and Collins were looking pretty tired out and impatient.

# CHAPTER XV

"It took a mighty long time to find that rope," says Collins, sort of cross-like.

"It's a long rope," I says. "The longer the rope the longer it takes to find it. I could 'a' had a short one here half an hour ago."

The rope was in a coil, which made it easy to throw. I sent it sailing over to Mark, who caught it and went to work making a lasso out of it. He was as deliberate as if we were sitting on a shady porch and not perched out there with the sun beating down on our heads like it wanted to melt us down to butter.

"Hurry it up," says I, "or there won't be anything left of me to get down. I'll melt and run off."

"When you go to make a l-l-lasso," says Mark, "make a good one. It's b-better to take a minnit or two extry than to have the knot s-s-slip and let the dog loose."

There was something to that, all right—I'd rather be sunburnt than dog-bit. He got it done at last, but then he took his time making just the right-sized noose and coiling the rope so it suited him to a tee. When everything was fixed so he was satisfied he came to the end of the roof and called over to me.

"P-p-poke him with your pole," says he.

I knew what he wanted—it was to have the dog rear up so he could toss the noose over its body, and I got my pole. The dog seemed to be real interested in me and showed his teeth. When I shoved the pole at him he just rose right up and announced himself, and his announcement wasn't friendly to me. I jerked back the pole, and he stood on his hind legs to reach it. Then Mark Tidd threw his lasso. The first shot he made it. The noose plopped down over Mr. Doggie's fore legs and head and was jerked tight around his ribs. You never saw an animal look so surprised as he did just as Mark flopped him over. From the ground he looked around at me sort of surprised and hurt, as much as to say I didn't play fair. Well, I thought, neither did he. He'd bite, and I wouldn't.

Mark fastened the rope, and we all got down. I was glad it was a strong rope, for that bulldog acted like he'd have busted one just a little weaker. He did his best, and we couldn't expect any more of him than that. My! how he pulled and jerked! We were sorry to leave him fastened up, but there wasn't any other way out of it, so we said good-by to him as politely as we could and went out of the farm-yard.

"Milk," says Collins, "and pie. Um! Good, weren't they? Let's stop at every farm-house we see."

Jiggins and Mark hadn't a word to say.

I lagged behind, and pretty soon Mark dropped back with me.

"What d'you think I found in that barn?" I says.

"Rope," says he. "That's what you went a-after."

"I found somethin' else."

"Well," says he, "what was it?"

"Alfred," I says. "Alfred Bell! Horse! Uncle Hieronymous Alphabet Bell's horse!"

"What?" he says, so astonished he stopped still in his tracks.

"Sure's shootin'," I told him.

"It's all right, then," says he. "We don't need to w-w-worry any more."

"I should think we ought to worry more than ever."

"'Course not. He'll get your note, prob'ly t-to-night. That'll set him on his guard."

"What note?" I asked, feeling a sort of sinking in my stomach.

"Why," says he, "the one you pinned on the stall where he'd be sure to see it."

Now what do you think of that? Of course that was what I should have done, and it would have ended the battle right there, but I never thought of it. It was so plain to see, Mark thought of course I'd done it. I never was so ashamed in my life as when I had to tell him I didn't.

"Well," says he, heaving his fat shoulders, "we know your uncle's near, any-how." Then he sort of sighed. "Too b-b-bad I can't be everywhere," he says, and that was all. He never spoke another word of blame. Mark Tidd never wasted much time crying over spilt milk.

"We got to escape t-t-to-night, sure," says he.

"Yes," says I.

"And," says he, "we got to fix it so we d-d-don't go far to-day. We got to l-lay up the expedition."

"How?" I asked.

"Dun'no'," says he. "We'll wait for a streak of l-l-luck."

It was noon by the time we got back to the boats, and, naturally, Jiggins and Mark insisted we should have dinner right then and there. Nobody objected much. That took up about an hour, and then we wasted another hour resting and fussing around. But Collins insisted on our getting started at last. We went the same way as before—Jiggins and Mark in the flatboat, and Collins with me in the canoe.

We paddled along, not saying much, for an hour. My back ached, and I wished I was ashore lying under a tree. So did Collins, by the look of him. Nothing hap-pened except turtles flopping into the water off logs, or birds flying overhead. The only noise was the flow of the water, and we were so used to that by this time we didn't notice it any more. It was like the tick of a clock. Did you ever sit in the room with a clock and try to see if you could hear it tick? Well, just try it sometime. Mostly folks are so accustomed to the sound that it sort of stops being a sound and gets to be a part of one sound made up of a lot of little ones. I know I've had to try hard and put all my attention to it before I could make out the ticking. And that's the way it was with the river.

The banks of the river kept getting higher and higher until we came to a bend where the river widened out into a sort of pool with a backwater, and up from this rose a bluff higher than anything we'd seen. At the foot of this bluff was a little flat of sand that drifted down and stuck there, and on the edge was a mess of drift-wood and logs. The most interesting things, though, were an old boat-house and a tiny shanty that stood on the flat. No, they weren't the most interesting, though I did think so for a spell. The really interesting thing was a big, fat woodchuck that was feeding not twenty feet from the boat-house up on the side of the hill.

I yelled at him. He turned and looked for all the world like he was scowling at us. Then he ducked into the boat-house and disappeared.

"B-bet his hole's in there," Mark Tidd yelled. "Let's go ashore and see."

Everybody was willing to rest, so we ran ashore and drew up the navy. The boathouse wasn't at the water's edge like you might think, but stood back on the sand, maybe twenty feet from the water. It looked as if it had been washed there by the flood-water in the spring. The other shanty, a little thing about four feet square, was a fish-shanty, Mark said. It didn't have any floor in half of it. The other half was mostly seat and sheet-iron stove.

"They p-pull it onto the ice," says Mark. "Then they chop out a h-hole and sit there and spear fish. It's dark in the shanty, so they can s-s-see down into the water."

It looked easy. All the man who owned it had to do was sit on that seat and wait for a fish to swim past him, then he up with his spear and let her go. I bet it was fun.

We went to the boat-house next, and there, sure enough, was the woodchuck's hole. It was at the far end of the house and went down at an angle into the side of the bluff.

"Poke him out," says Collins.

"Nothin' to poke with," says Mark.

Jiggins came crowding in to see what there was to see, and he said to go out and get a pole or something.

"Not much chance," he says. "Hole too deep. Try, though. Woodchuck's good to eat. Fat."

Mark motioned to me, and we both went outside.

"B-B-Binney," says Mark, his little eyes twinkling like they always do when he's excited. "It l-l-looks like we got 'em." My, how he stuttered!

"How?" says I.

"Watch me and h-help," says he.

He brought a small log or a big pole, I don't know which to call it.

"Git over by the door," he says, pointing to the heavy door of the boat-house that stood wide open. "Stand right there, where they c-c-can't see you. When I whistle you p-p-push the door shut. Not slow. Fast. B-b-bang it!"

I saw it in a second. He was planning to shut up Jiggins and Collins in the boat-house while we got away. I did like he said, and braced myself to slam.

He whistled, I slammed. The door started sort of hard, but it moved, and I made it move fast. *Bang!* it went shut, and *slam* went Mark's leg against it. That locked Mr. Door, I can tell you. One end of the log was wedged in the sand and the other forced against the door. It would have taken an elephant to move it. But Mark wasn't satisfied. He propped it shut with two more logs and then dragged a shorter and thicker piece right in front. The door was pretty nearly covered up before we were through.

Mark straightened up and grinned then. "Hello, inside," says he.

"What's this? Let us out! Quick!" says Jiggins.

"C-c-couldn't do it p-possibly," says Mark. "Have to dig out, I guess. 'Twon't take l-long. G-g-good-by."

They began to holler like anything, but we didn't stop. At the boats Mark told me to push off the canoe while he tended to the flatboat. He tended to it, all right—with a big stone.

He didn't have to drop that stone on the bottom of the boat but once. Two planks busted.

Mark climbed into the canoe with me, and we dug in our paddles.

"H-h-hurry," says he; but he didn't need to tell me. I was hurrying as hard as I could. I wanted to get as much distance between Jiggins & Co. and us as possible. They were nice men, but I didn't want any more of their company till we'd had a little chat with Uncle Hieronymous.

For the first time I had a chance to draw a breath and do a little thinking. Then it began to dawn on me what Mark had done. All in a second he'd seen his chance, and just as quick he took advantage of it. I would have sat around that boat-house all day without scheming to shut up the enemy in it, but not Mark. It didn't matter what he saw, he always tried to fit it into his plans. I suppose he began studying about that boat-house as soon as it came into sight, and by the time we landed his plan was all ready.

Wasn't it easy, though? All he had to do was get Jiggins and Collins in there alone. That was all. It doesn't look very hard, and it didn't seem to be hard. But the brainy part was thinking it up in a second and working it when there wasn't a chance in the world the enemy would be expecting anything.

Take Marcus Aurelius Fortunatus Tidd by and large, and it looks to me like he was considerable of a general.

# CHAPTER XVI

From now on so many things happened, one right onto the heels of the other, that it's a little confusing to remember them all and get them in the right places. It doesn't seem as if I stopped to breathe for about a month. Only, the whole thing was over in a night and less than a day. But it was a night and a day a fellow couldn't forget if he lived to be a million years old.

That first thing that happened was the noise. Mark and I had been paddling about three quarters of an hour when we heard it first.

"Bridge ahead," I says. "Hear that rig goin' across?"

Mark didn't say anything, but I could see, by the way he tipped his head to one side, he was listening careful. We paddled on for ten minutes, and the noise came again. It was a sort of mix-up of rattle and rumble and roar. It sounded to me like a team crossing a bridge, but, after all, it didn't sound quite like it.

"'Tain't a b-b-bridge," says Mark.

"What is it, then?"

"Dun'no'," says he.

Pretty soon it went off again. Rattle, rattle, rumble, rumble, clatter, clatter, with a sort of squeal twisted in for good measure.

"S-some kind of a machine," says Mark.

It kept coming every little while, sometimes as much as twenty minutes apart, and growing louder every time it came.

"S-sounds like a machine," says Mark.

That's what it was, but, when you come to think of it, it was a funny sort of a machine, and funny things were being done with it. About half past four we came slap onto it. It was a big scow more than fifty feet long and twenty or so wide. A flat, square house covered about two-thirds of it, and a whopping big derrick stuck up near the front end. There was a smoke-stack, so we knew there must be an engine. We'd have found that out pretty quick, anyhow, because it was hissing and fussing and spluttering away, and steam was spurting out of the side every little while.

A big cable stretched from the boom of the derrick up-stream, and the end of it was hitched to two of the biggest timbers I ever saw. They were hewn square, and each of them must have been sixty feet long. They were fastened side by side into a raft that would have floated an elephant. There were two men on it. I didn't pay special attention to them, because I was so interested in the raft, but Mark did. I heard him let his breath go in the whoppingest sigh of relief a man ever heaved.

"We've d-d-done it," says he.

"What?" says I.

"Won," says he. "We've f-f-found your uncle. There's Ole and Jerry."

I almost tipped over the canoe, I turned so quick to look. Sure enough, there were Ole and Jerry working like big beavers. One was at one end of the raft, and the other was at the other end. They had big pike-poles and were pushing the contraption up-stream. It wasn't any easy job, either. When we saw them first they were about a hundred feet away from the scow. They poled as far as they could without turning the bend, and then went ashore and fastened their raft to a tree with chains. When that was done Ole waved his hand to the engineer, and right there the queerest piece of traveling I ever saw was done. I don't see how anybody ever thought it up. The engineer started his engine and began winding in the cable. Of course, because the far end of it was fast, that pulled the scow ahead. That wasn't so outlandish, though. It was the steering! Would you believe it, but that engineer steered up-stream with the boom of the derrick. He'd swing that back and forth, all the time reeling in, and by moving the spot where the strain came first to one side and then to the other he steered as straight as you please. If the big scow started to veer over to the left the engineer would throw the boom way over to the right, and the pull of the cable would straighten her up. I never saw Mark look more tickled with anything in his life. He actually looked *jealous*. I knew what he was thinking—it was a big wish that he'd been the fellow to think up that scheme.

Neither Mark nor I said a word to Ole and Jerry till the scow had eaten up all its cable again. It reminded you of a spider. You've seen a spider going up, up to the ceiling by eating its own thread. But when the boat stopped we both yelled at once.

Ole and Jerry straightened up, rested their pike-poles on the bottom, and stared at us out of big, round, surprised blue eyes. They didn't say a word. We paddled over.

"Where's Uncle Hieronymous?" I asked, so excited I couldn't sit still.

Ole looked at Jerry, and Jerry looked at Ole. Then both of them looked at us. Pretty soon Ole spoke.

"Py Jimminy!" says he to Jerry.

Jerry wagged his head and grinned at Mark. "She bane that fat boy," he says.

"Yass," says Ole. "She bane him." Then they both threw back their heads and laughed so loud they must have frightened birds a quarter of a mile away.

"Where's Uncle Hieronymous?" I asked again.

They didn't pay a bit of attention to me, but kept on looking at us and at each other.

"They come in a leetle boat," says Ole.

"Yass, in leetle boat."

"Down the river," says Ole.

"Sure. She bane come down dat river. Two poy. Py Jimminy!"

"Where's Uncle Hieronymous?" I asked again, getting sort of mad. Nobody likes to ask questions and get no attention paid them. But Ole and Jerry seemed to think it was so funny we should come down the river in a little boat they didn't have much time to give answers. After a while they did answer, though.

"Hieronymous?" says Ole. "Oh, yass. He bane work here."

Jerry bobbed his head. "Sure. He work here."

"Is he on that scow?" I suppose we might have saved a lot of time by going there to see, but we didn't.

"Scow?" Jerry had to scratch his head over that. Ole scratched his head, too, and then they looked at each other and grinned as foolish as a couple of babies.

"Dey came for see Hieronymous," says Ole; and then he had to laugh again like there was a funny joke.

"Ay tank so," says Jerry. "Ay tank dey want for see him."

"Yes," says I, "we do. Is he there?"

"He work here," says Ole. "He come with us here."

"Yass," says Jerry.

"But," says Ole, and then he had to stop to laugh again, "he bane gone off now."

"Yass," says Jerry, "he bane gone off."

I suppose that's what they thought was so comical.

Well, sir, that took us right between wind and water, as the old privateering stories say. We thought the fight was over and we'd won, and here, when there didn't seem to be another thing to do, Uncle Hieronymous had up and gone away. I crumpled up in the boat and felt like crying.

"Wh-where did he go?" Mark asked. It was the first time he had spoken.

"Go? He go dis mornin'," says Ole.

"Nine-ten o'clock," says Jerry.

"But where? Where d-d-did he go?"

"Oh-ho!" says Jerry. "Haw-haw! Listen, Ole. You hear dat?"

"Haw-haw!" says Ole. "I hear. She bane talk funny, eh?"

"Talk some more again," says Jerry.

Mark was red as a beet, and I expected to hear him tear right into them and tell them what for, but he didn't. I guess he knew they didn't mean any harm and weren't even trying to be rude. They were just interested.

"Do you know wh-wh-where he went?" Mark asked again.

"Ludington," says Ole.

"Yass," says Jerry, "Ludington."

"When is he coming back?" I wanted to know.

"Oh, two-t'ree day," says Ole.

"Maybe t'ree-four," says Jerry.

"He go wid day boss," says Ole.

"Yass," says Jerry, "wid day boss."

There wasn't any use trying to get anything out of those Swedes, so we let go and paddled down to the scow to see if the engineer wasn't more likely to be useful. He was a short man with spectacles and not much hair. It was a habit of his to keep his head on one side and look at you over the rims of his spectacles in the mournfulest way you can imagine. He was mournful all over; every line there was in his face sort of drooped, especially the corners of his mouth, which looked like there was danger of their slipping some day and going *slam!* off his jaw. He looked like an owl that had its feelings hurt.

He was leaning against the door of the engine-room when we came alongside, looking down at us as if he thought maybe he'd have to cry pretty soon.

"G-g-good afternoon," says Mark.

The engineer walked to the side of the boat, working his lower jaw like he was chewing something, which he wasn't at all. He stood a minnit without saying a word, then, in the dolefulest voice you ever heard, he says:

"If I was to git into that pesky boat it 'u'd be jest my luck to git tipped over."

We never got to know him very well, but in the little time we were with him we found out that was just the way he looked at things. So far as we found out he never had anything very awful happen to him, but he didn't have any faith in his luck, and he was certain-sure the next thing he did was going to turn out bad.

"We want to know about Uncle Hieronymous," I says.

"Who be you?" he asked. "I don't calc'late to spread news about anybody until I find out who I'm tellin'. You might mean some harm to Hieronymous."

"He's my uncle," I says. "We boys are staying at his house for the summer."

He drew down his mouth till it was near a foot long. "Well," says he, "why don't you stay there, then, instid of gallivantin' around the country in a boat that hain't much short of bein' murderous?"

"Because," says Mark, "we g-g-got to see him special and important."

"Anythin' unfort'nate happened him?" asked the engineer, leaning over the edge of the scow. It looked like misfortunes were a regular specialty of his.

"No," says Mark, "but somethin's goin' to if we don't find him p-p-pretty quick."

"You don't tell," says the engineer, and he come close to smiling.

"Ole says he's gone to Ludington," I says.

"That's where he's gone, and I hope nothin' unfort'nate comes of it. I didn't noways like the look of that hoss the boss drove."

"Well," says Mark, "we g-g-got to git to Ludington fast. What's the quickest way?"

"There hain't none," says the engineer. "It'll take you a day by river, pervidin' you don't git tipped over and drownded. It's two miles to Scottville and eight from there to Ludington, by land, and you hain't got no hoss. Them's the two ways, and neither of 'em the quickest."

"Isn't there a train from Scottville to Ludington?"

"Yes," says he, "but I wouldn't risk my neck on it. Not never. I wouldn't git onto that train of cars no more'n I'd git into one of these here autymobiles."

"Can we come aboard?" I says, after a minnit. "It's pretty cramped down here, and I'd like to sit on somethin' comfortable a few minnits."

"Yes," says Mark, "and we wouldn't git m-m-mad at you if you offered us somethin' to eat."

"Come ahead," says the engineer, "but be careful. I can't swim, so don't go dependin' on me to haul you out if you fall in."

We scrambled aboard and sat down in a couple of rickety kitchen chairs. The engineer watched us awhile, chewing away at nothing, and then, wrinkling up his face, says:

"What might your names be? I don't rec'lect hearin' 'em."

"My name's M-M-Mark Tidd, and his is Binney Jenks."

"Huh! Mark Tidd! That hain't no kind of a name. It's jest a sort of a snort. There hain't enough of it."

"Well," says I, "his whole name is Marcus Aurelius Fortunatus Tidd. I calc'late that's plenty long."

"Sam Hill!" says the engineer. "Sam Hill! Who ever heard the like! Honest, is that his name?"

"Honest Injun."

"It 'u'd make me nervous. It's the kind of a name you see in the papers. Somehow it brings to mind pieces in the newspapers about train-wrecks or trouble or somethin'. No, sir, I wouldn't think it was safe to have a name like that."

"What kind of a name do you l-l-like?" Mark asked.

"There's my own. It hain't a lucky name, so to speak, but it hain't never been no detriment. My name," says he, "is Wednesday Hogtoter."

I most tumbled off my chair. "What?" I says, not believing my ears.

"Wednesday Hogtoter," he repeated. "Hogtoter, bein' my father's name, become mine natural-like. Wednesday was the day my father up and took a prize to the state fair for raisin' the biggest potaters in the state. He deemed that day consid'able of a day, so he give it to me for a name."

Mark Tidd was sniffing. I knew what that meant—something to eat. When I came to sniff a little myself I noticed coffee. My, but it smelled good! There was other things in the air, like bacon, and I thought I could pick out the odor of hot biscuits.

Mark looked at his watch.

"What time is it?" I asked.

He didn't answer me, but asked a question of Mr. Hogtoter. "What t-t-time d'you eat?" he says.

"Half past five," says Mr. Hogtoter.

Mark sighed. "Twenty minutes yet," he says, and sank back, looking gloomier than all-git-out.

"Can we look at the engine?" I asked Mr. Hogtoter.

He allowed we could, so we went in the engine-room, but there wasn't much to see. We came out again in a minnit to watch Mr. Hogtoter steer the scow upstream again with the boom.

At last the cook came out and hollered, "Grub-pile!" which meant it was suppertime. Ole and Jerry came on the run, and Mark and I didn't wait for a written invitation. It's lucky they had lots to eat on board, or somebody would have come out at the little end of the horn. I ate and ate, and Mark ate and ate *and* ate. He was still going it when the rest were through.

The cook shook his head. "Wouldn't board you permanent, young feller, for twice my wages," says he. "Is this the first time you've et this year?"

Mark just grinned. He was full now, and that made him feel good. He never cared much, anyhow, when folks made fun of his appetite.

We settled back in our chairs; and I was just getting ready to ask more about the way to Ludington when somebody hollered outside. I knew that voice in a minnit. It was Jiggins.

# CHAPTER XVII

For a minnit I was scared, and even Mark Tidd looked kind of blue around the gills, as dad says. But then I thought Ole and Jerry and Mr. Hogtoter wouldn't let Collins and Jiggins take us off the scow, so I quit being frightened.

Ole got up and poked his head out of the door.

"Hello!" says Jiggins again. "Seen a couple of boys in a canoe?"

Ole turned around to us and grinned, then he called to Jiggins, "Ay tank so."

"How long ago?"

"Ay tank one hour."

Then I heard Collins say something in an undertone.

"Good idea," says Jiggins. "Do no harm. May do some good. I'll ask him." Then he called up to Ole: "D'you know Mr. Bell—Hieronymous Alphabet Bell?"

"Ay tank ay know him," says Ole.

"Know where he is?" asked Jiggins.

Mark jumped to his feet. "Don't—" he started to say to Ole.

But for once the big Swede answered right off without any fooling. "He bane go to Ludington."

"When?"

"Nine-ten o'clock."

Mark was banging Ole on the back. "Don't tell him any m-m-more," says he. "They're enemies. They're t-t-tryin' to smouge Uncle Hieronymous's mine." Then he ran right out on deck.

"G-g-go on away," says he. "You can't f-find out any more. You're b-beat!"

"Well, I swan!" says Jiggins. "Howdy, Mark. Hard work gettin' out of that boat-house. Had to find another boat. But here we are."

Sure enough, they did have another boat. They must have found it somewhere along the river near the boat-house.

Jiggins didn't seem to be much discouraged. "Well," says he, "we enjoyed your company. Sure we did. Nice boy. Brains. Always liked boys with brains—especially fat boys. Good-by. Ludington, eh? He's in Ludington. Well, Mark Tidd, we're off for Ludington. Beat, eh? Not yet. Not yet." They pushed off their boat and started down-stream. "Good-by," says Jiggins again. "I'll give your regards to

Uncle Hieronymous. Good-by."

Mark didn't wait a minnit. "G-g-got to beat 'em to Ludington," says he. "No time to waste." He thought a minnit. "When does the t-t-train leave Scottville?"

"Long about nine o'clock," says Mr. Hogtoter.

"How far's Scottville?"

"Two mile."

"H-h-how do we get there?"

"Walk," says Mr. Hogtoter. "There's a road back there a spell." He jerked his thumb up the bank. "But they'll beat you. You'll git lost or somethin'."

"What time is it?"

"Half past six."

Mark thought and pinched his cheek. "That g-gives us two hours and a half," says he. "Come on, Binney. Will s-s-somebody show us the road?"

"Ay tank ay show you," says Ole.

"Ay tank ay show you, too," says Jerry.

"Come on, then," Mark says, quick. "We can't l-lose any time."

We said good-by to Mr. Hogtoter, and I told him I hoped he wouldn't have any bad luck. He said he was expecting some every minnit, and he said, too, he was sure we were in for some.

"Be careful," says he. "Not that bein' careful is any good. If you're goin' to have misfortune, takin' care don't help a bit. Never helped me. Looks to me like Hieronymous was in for misfortune."

We climbed the bank with Ole and Jerry, and, not having either time or breath to say anything, we made off across the fields toward the road without any talk. It was maybe a quarter of a mile.

"You find Scottville now, ay tank," says Ole.

"Sure," says Jerry, "ay tank so, too."

"Good-by," says Mark, "and m-much obliged."

"Good-by," says Ole and Jerry, and then we were off alone. Once I looked back. They were still standing where we left them, laughing as hard as they could laugh. There isn't a bit of doubt they thought Mark Tidd was the funniest person they ever saw.

We walked as fast as we could, and got to Scottville in plenty of time. Mark bought the tickets, because he had the money. We had elected him treasurer, so he had all there was. Then we sat down on the depot platform to wait for the train. It was getting dusk, which turned out to be a pretty lucky thing for us. It was lucky, too, that we were sitting near a corner of the depot. In spite of Mr. Hogtoter we were having good luck for a while, anyhow.

Just as the train whistled down the track somebody came through the depot door. It was Jiggins. Collins was right at his heels. They turned to look down the track in the direction away from us, and right there I gave Mark Tidd the hardest shove he ever got. It toppled him off the bench. I jumped over him and around the corner. Right off he knew something was up, so he scrambled after me.

"Collins and Jiggins," says I.

"No n-n-need to bust my neck," says Mark.

"How'd they git here?"

"Walked, most likely. Asked s-s-somebody how to get to Ludington."

"How do we git there now?"

Mark looked at me disgusted. "On the t-train, of course."

"But they'll see us."

"M-m-maybe not," says he. "Anyhow, we got to take the chance."

The train came banging in in a few minnits. We watched Jiggins and Collins get aboard and took particular pains to see what car they sat in. It was the forward coach.

"Come on," says Mark.

He went to the last coach and climbed on. So did I. We walked right through and stood on the back platform.

"If the conductor'll l-l-let us stay here," says Mark, "we'll be all right."

The train started up. Eight miles to go! That wasn't far. Even on that railroad it oughtn't to take more than a quarter of an hour. But even a quarter of an hour on the same train with Collins and Jiggins was too long. Jiggins was an uncertain person. You never could depend on him to stay in his seat. He might take a notion any time to come wandering around the train, and then, like as not, he'd find us.

"What'll we do if they come onto us?" I asked him.

"Dun'no'," says he. "Nothin', I guess."

After a while we saw the conductor coming through the car. I put my head in the door and held out our tickets. He frowned at us, and I thought he was going to make us come inside, but all he did was say to be careful. We allowed we'd do that.

I looked at my watch and saw five minnits were gone by. That was a third of the ride. The air was full of dust and grit and smoke, but through it all we could feel the coolness of Lake Michigan. I never had seen Lake Michigan or any other big lake, and I was anxious to. Mark said it would look just like the ocean. Anyhow, it sent a dandy soft coolness back into the country, and we were much obliged.

Another five minnits went past, and then we began to see lights every little while.

"Must be g-gettin' near," says Mark.

Pretty soon we could stretch our necks around the corner of the car and see lots of lights ahead, some of them up in the air. We knew these were street-lights and that we were getting into Ludington. Then we passed some factory buildings and began to pat ourselves on the back that we were there safe. The train slackened down until it wasn't going very fast.

"We're here," says I to Mark.

"I see you are," says somebody, and I turned quick to look. It was Jiggins grinning at us out of the door.

"Howdy?" says he. "Lucky I came back here, eh? To be sure. Didn't think I'd see you again."

I looked at Mark. He didn't wait for another word, but just stepped down onto the lowest step of the car and jumped off into the dark. Jiggins sort of jumped past me and made a grab after him, and then, not knowing anything better to do myself, I jumped off the train on the other side and struck the sand of the right of way. For a few seconds I was so busy twisting head over heels and banging and scraping myself that I didn't have any time to think about anybody else. I landed with a bump. For a minnit I laid there without being able to make up my mind how fatally I was hurt, but I found out I could move every one of my arms and legs and that nothing was the matter with me at all. Then I got up to look for Mark.

I found him about fifty feet back, sitting flat on the ground, with his legs stretched out in front of him. I expect he landed that way. If he did it wasn't any fun, and it was pretty lucky nobody happened to be resting where he struck. If there had been we'd 'a' had to dig him out of the ground, Mark would have driven him in so deep.

"Good evenin'," says I, make-believe polite.

"Umph!" says he, and waggled his head.

"Git up," says I. "They'll be comin' in a second."

He groaned again and got onto his feet. I took him by the arm and dragged him off the right of way into the dark. Not far away we found a street and started up it, hoping it would bring us out some place we wanted to be.

"Now," says Mark, "to f-f-find Uncle Hieronymous."

That was more difficult than we had any idea of.

# CHAPTER XVIII

There we were in a town we never saw before, with no place to go and no idea what to do next. Ludington seemed to us like a pretty big town after Wicksville, but we didn't let that frighten us.

"What'll we do now?" I asked.

"I'm g-g-goin' to git the gravel out of my ears," says Mark. "You can do whatever you want to."

That *was* a pretty good idea. The gravel I got wasn't in my ears; mostly it was down my neck. I was full of it. I don't suppose the railroad company ever missed what I took away, and I didn't see any reason why I should carry it back, so I left a nice little pile of it on the sidewalk.

"Wish I could wash up," says Mark.

"And I," I says, cross-like, "wish you'd quit thinkin' about how uncomfortable you are and start to thinkin' about Uncle Hieronymous."

"Binney," says he, "d-d-don't get het up. Think a minnit. Jiggins and Collins never saw Uncle Hieronymous, did they? Then they wouldn't know him if they met him. And they d-don't know where to look. They'll never find him to-night. There hain't such an awful hurry that I c-c-can't get the gravel out of my hair."

"I'll bet they're lookin' for him right now."

Mark sighed. "There hain't any use in it," says he, "but I s'pose I g-g-got to humor you. Come on."

We went straight ahead till we came to a wide street with electric lights on it. Down to the right you could see stores and business buildings, so we turned that way, and a walk of three or four blocks took us downtown.

"Now," says Mark, "where do we b-b-begin lookin' for him?"

"Hotel," says I, pointing across the street to one.

Mark looked. "No use askin' there," he says. "Uncle Hieronymous wouldn't stay there."

"Why?" I asked.

"Two reasons," says he. "In the f-f-first place, he wouldn't take any comfort eatin' his meals there, and, in the s-second place, it costs too much. Uncle Hieronymous wouldn't eat in any b-big dinin'-room with f-f-fifty folks lookin' on."

"What kind of a place would he stop at?"

"Either a boardin'-house or a leetle f-f-farmer's hotel. I b-bet there's an old hotel here s-s-somewheres where he would f-feel to home, one where there hain't much s-s-style."

"Well," says I, "s'pose we find out."

We wandered around and found a couple of hotels that didn't look too fine. In both of them we asked for Uncle Hieronymous, and both times the man behind the counter grinned when we mentioned the name.

"Say," says the last one, "what's that feller been doin'? Lots of folks lookin' for him to-night."

"What's that?" Mark asked.

"Two fellers in here not twenty minnits ago askin' for him."

"A f-f-fat one and a thin one?"

"Them's the pair."

Mark and I looked at each other. It was dead certain Collins and Jiggins weren't letting any grass grow under their feet.

"They might stumble onto him," I says.

"Yes," says Mark, "and they m-m-might stumble onto us, too."

I never thought of that. We might run bang into them any time, and then what would happen? Something would, that's sure; but what? I didn't want to find out.

"We got to go cautious," says I.

Mark wrinkled his nose scornful-like.

"How'd you come to think of that?" he asked, snappish. I guess that tumble off the train had upset his disposition. I made up my mind I'd leave him alone till he felt better.

After a while he stopped still in the middle of the sidewalk and says, "Hang it!" You never saw such a disgusted look as he had on his face.

"What's matter?" I asked.

"I ought to be k-k-kicked," says he.

"All right," says I. "What for?"

"For not askin' who Uncle Hieronymous w-w-worked for."

To be sure. Neither of us had thought of it. It would have been as easy as biting an apple to find him if we knew who his boss was, but we didn't. Now there wasn't any way of finding out. Mark felt pretty bad. He said he guessed he was getting feeble-minded and a lot of things like that. And he was mad, too. I was glad to see that, for when Marcus Aurelius Fortunatus Tidd gets mad you want to look out. From now on Jiggins & Co. would have to travel pretty fast to beat us.

About fifteen minutes later I saw Jiggins and Collins about a block ahead.

"There," says I to Mark, "is the enemy."

"F-f-fine," says he. "Come on."

"Where?"

"F-follow 'em, of course. If they find Uncle Hieronymous we can b-bust in on 'em. If they go to b-bed we'll be able to get some sleep, too."

That was a fact. So long as we knew they were in bed it would be safe for us to take a rest, and if they were to find my uncle with us looking on it would be pretty funny if there wasn't some way for us to warn him before he signed any papers and made over his mineral rights. It looked, as Mark said, like we occupied a pretty fine strategical position. He knows a lot of words like that, and you ought to hear him say them. On a good long word with "s's" in it like "strategical," he'll hiss and stutter and splutter for five minutes. It's better than listening to a phonograph.

We kept about half a block behind Jiggins & Co. and on the other side of the road, taking pains to keep people between us and the men. We watched them go into several places, probably to ask about Uncle Hieronymous, but every time they came out disappointed. Finally they stopped and argued a few minutes, and then wheeled suddenly and came back toward us. The streets were pretty clear by this time, and there was no chance for us to mingle with the crowd and get away. All we could do was duck into a dark stairway.

Jiggins & Co. crossed the street to our side and came walking up the sidewalk slowly, like they were pretty well played out. If they felt anything like I did they were, and there's no doubt about it. Between falling off a train, paddling all day, and walking all the evening I felt like I was about ready to give up the ship. Another mile and I knew I'd up and splinter all to pieces on the sidewalk. Next day somebody'd have swept me up in a dust-pan and wondered where in the world all the slivers came from.

The nearer the enemy got the farther Mark and I scrooched back into the stairway. In a minnit they got right in front of us, and I heard Jiggins speak to somebody.

"Good evening, mister," he says.

"Good evening," says the stranger.

"We just came to town," says Jiggins. "Been here two hours. Walked and walked. Looking for a man. Old man. Lumberman. Know any lumbermen?"

"Heaps," says the stranger. "Used to be a lumber-jack myself."

"Just our man. I knew it as soon as I saw you. Says I, 'There's the feller.' Yes, sir. I said it just like that. Knows lots of lumbermen. Fine. The one we're looking for travels around carrying the name of Hieronymous Alphabet Bell. Know him? Old feller. Lives up Baldwin way."

"Sure I know Hieronymous," says the stranger. "Hain't seen him for months, but I know him. Him and me used to bunk together."

"He's in town. Came to-day. Can't find him. Where'd he be apt to be?"

"Well," says the stranger, "he'd be apt to be over to the Masonic Temple, but he hain't, 'cause I just come from there."

"Where does he usually stop?"

"Don't usually stop at all. Jest comes and goes."

Then he took to asking questions himself. "Friend of Hieronymous's be you?"

"Of course. To be sure. He hasn't two better friends."

"Never heard him mention you," says the stranger. "Lemme see. How long's Hieronymous's beard by now? Must be perty long, eh?"

"Never measured her exactly," says Jiggins. "Long, though. Foot, maybe. Great beard. Don't know when I ever saw a better one."

"Umph!" says the lumberman. "Good friends of Hieronymous's, eh? Perty intimate-like?"

"Well, not what you'd call intimate, maybe. But friends. Good friends."

"See him lately? Must 'a' seen him perty lately, eh?"

"Three days ago."

"Um!" says the stranger. "What was you lookin' for him for?"

"Business," says Jiggins, and his voice began to sound like he wasn't exactly pleased.

"Most likely," says the stranger. "Well," he says, sort of dry-like and humorous, "I don't calc'late I can help you any. Why? Best reason in the world. The Hieronymous I know don't wear no beard at all. Good evenin', gents."

Well, I could have busted right out laughing, but Mark pinched my leg so hard I almost hollered because it hurt. "Hush!" says he. Oh, but it was great! I never was so tickled in all my life as I was to hear that old lumberman get the best of those two. I'd pay money to hear it again. Yes, sir, I'd go as high as a quarter, and we don't dig up quarters in my back yard, either.

We waited a short spell, and Mark says: "I'll follow the lumberman and find out where Uncle Hieronymous is apt to be and who he w-w-works for. You f-f-follow Jiggins & Co. to where they sleep."

"All right," says I, and off we went.

Jiggins and Collins went straight to the big hotel on the avenue. I climbed the steps as close behind them as I dared and saw them go up to the man behind the counter. This man poked a big book at them, and they signed their names to it. Then the man called a boy over, who took a key and led them over to the stairs. All this time I was peeking in a window with a screen in it.

Just as Jiggins was putting his foot on the first step he turned around and called out, "Leave a call for us for seven o'clock."

That settled them for the night. I knew where they were, and I knew how long they would stay there. Now Mark and I could take a few hours' snooze, and we needed it bad, I can tell you. I can't think of anything I wouldn't have traded for eight long hours of sleep.

I went back to the corner of the street where Mark had gone after the lumberman and waited there. In fifteen minutes he came limping along, looking as tired and disconsolate-like as if he was just getting in from a seven-days' journey and somebody had stolen his clothes the last day out.

"Well?" says I.

He shook his head. "Not much g-g-good," says he. "He don't know who Uncle Hieronymous works for, and he d-d-don't know where he is. P-promised to tell him we were here if he saw him."

"Well," says I, "Jiggins & Co. are tucked in their little beds and won't be out till seven o'clock to-morrow. Have you got any good arguments why *we* shouldn't find a place to sleep?"

"N-n-nary argument," says Mark.

"Where'll we go?"

"Let's t-try that little hotel back yonder. The one with the b-b-balcony in front."

"All right," says I. "Have we got money enough?"

"I've g-got five dollars and thirty-two c-c-cents," says he.

That looked like it would be enough, so we went back to the little hotel and stirred up the man, who was fast asleep behind his counter. He made us pay a dollar in advance, because he said we didn't have any baggage. He grinned then and said he didn't calc'late we looked over-trustworthy. Said we looked to him like we were dangerous characters and ought to be watched, and made a great clatter about locking up his little safe. There are a lot of men who think it's awful funny to make fun of boys that way. I've known men who never got a joke on a grown man that were always picking onto kids. But this fellow picked on the wrong kid. Mark stood it awhile, getting more and more provoked every second. At last he lays down the dollar and says:

"There, mister, now you g-g-got somethin' to put in your safe. Bet this d-d-dollar'll s'prise it most to death."

Well, sir, that's the way that hotel looked, like dollars were pretty scarce there, and what Mark said hit the man right under the belt. At first he was mad, but pretty soon he grinned, sheepish-like, and says:

"You got me there, sonny. You got me there. Business hain't what it used to be when the river was floatin' down its millions of feet of timber. Them days is gone with 'em. There's new things to-day, boys, but us old-timers hain't able somehow to learn new ways. Our luck went with the timber. Don't blame you for hittin' back, sonny. I was perty fresh with you, and I beg your pardon." He stuck out his hand, and we both shook it, and were sorry for him. He looked like a nice man, and we hoped his hard luck wouldn't last.

He showed us up-stairs and came into the room with us.

"Never had no boys of my own," says he. "Wanted 'em, too." And he sat down and told us some stories about the old lumbering days and what a wild town Ludington was when the run came down and how the lumberjacks, with their Mackinaw jackets and calked boots, used to swarm into town and make it dangerous for anybody that couldn't take pretty good care of himself to be out of doors. He told us stories about the camps and about life on the rivers, and about fights and about birreling-matches, till we forgot we were sleepy. My, but those must have been bully days! But they're all over in Michigan. Men that thought too much of money have butchered off the pine, and there isn't any left, when it might have lasted for ever, almost, if it had been looked after the right way. The hotel-keeper says folks realize that now when it's too late.

After a while he said good night. "Boys," says he, "I've enjoyed talkin' with you. D'you know, I wouldn't charge you a cent for stoppin' here, but I bet I need that dollar a dozen times as bad as you do."

# CHAPTER XIX

The hotel-keeper called us at six o'clock. There wasn't any need for a second call, and we hurried down and had some eggs and salt pork and potatoes and coffee and bread and butter and canned peaches. Just a light breakfast. After we got out in the street we bought some bananas and ate three apiece. After that we felt all right.

"To-day's the l-l-last of it," says Mark.

"Somebody'll win sure before night," I says.

"It'll be us," he says.

That's what a good breakfast will do for a fellow. It gives him confidence.

We started off for the hotel where Jiggins & Co. were and sat down on the porch where we could look into the office and see them the minnit they came down-stairs. We waited and waited. After a while the clock struck seven.

"They're due now," I says.

But they didn't come. At half past seven I began to get fidgety and so did Mark.

"Don't seem l-l-like they'd oversleep to-day," says he.

"It don't," says I.

"Let's investigate," says he.

We marched in to the man behind the counter and asked for Mr. Jiggins.

"Fat man?" he asked.

"Yes."

"He and his friend got up early," says the man. "They left a call for seven, but they were down here at six. Had breakfast and went out."

Now, that was a nice thing to start the day with, wasn't it? We thought we had the advantage of them. It was all plain as pie to us how we could stick to their heels till they found Uncle Hieronymous and then bust in on them and knock their scheme a-kiting. Now the shoe was pinching the other foot, and it pinched hard.

We turned away without so much as saying thank you to the man. Somehow there didn't seem to be much to thank him for. It would have been too much like saying much obliged to a cow that hooked you. Out on the porch we flopped down in a couple of chairs and looked at each other.

"Looks like we was done for," I says.

Mark Tidd never will admit he's beaten. It made him mad to hear me say so.

"I'll sh-sh-show you if we're b-b-beat," he says, stuttering so bad he almost choked. "We hain't beat, and we hain't goin' to be b-b-beat."

"All right," says I, "that suits me fine. How do we manage it?"

"Sittin' here won't do it," says he, and got onto his feet. "Come on."

There wasn't a thing to do but try to find uncle ourselves. If we got to him before Jiggins & Co. all right. If they found him first the bacon was burned, and there we were. Nice, wasn't it? It made me sick to think of all the work we'd done and all the trouble we'd taken, and then to have the whole thing depend on luck at the end. We were discouraged, but we didn't let up. We said we'd keep up the battle till the cows came home, and we did.

I never saw a man so hard to find as Uncle Hieronymous was. We met men who had seen him, and we went into places where he'd been, but nobody knew where he'd gone or if he'd be back. This kept up till after ten o'clock.

"If he's h-h-hard for us to find," says Mark, "he must be hard for them to f-f-find."

There wasn't a great deal of comfort in that, but we took all we could get.

I saw by a jewelry-store clock it was a quarter to eleven, and just then a man spoke to Mark Tidd.

"Be you the kid that was askin' after Hieronymous Bell last night?"

"Yes," says Mark.

"I seen him," says the man; and then I recognized his voice. He was the lumberman that was talking with Jiggins & Co. the night before. "I seen him," says he, "with them two fellers, the fat one and the lean one. And there was another feller, too. Feller by the name of Siggins, lawyer. Not one of those here big lawyers that git to be judges, but a leetle one that goes slinkin' around corners. I calc'late he hain't no fit companion for Hieronymous."

"Where'd they g-g-go?" Mark asked, quick.

"Looked like they was headin' for Siggins's office."

"Where's that?"

The lumberman pointed to a yellow-brick building about a block back. "There," says he. "Up the stairs in a back room."

"M-much obliged," says Mark; and off we went hot-foot.

It was a case of hurry now, and hurry hard. Uncle Hieronymous was in the hands of the enemy, and his mine would be a goner if we didn't get our heavy artillery to work in a jiffy. But we had a chance, and a good one.

We ran. I beat Mark to the top of the stairs, but he was puffing right at my heels. How he did puff! The stairs came up in a hallway that ran straight ahead to the back of the building and an outside door. Another hall ran crossways from one end of the building to the other.

"Now, where's Siggins's o-o-office?" says Mark.

He got an answer, too. No sooner were the words out of his mouth than Collins stepped out of the door of the last office at the back of the building, the one on the left side of the hall. He saw us that very instant, and the way he came for us would have made a Comanche Indian proud. He swooped. I hadn't any idea he could move so fast. Before we could open our mouths he had us by the collars and was hustling us down-stairs. In less than a second we were out on the sidewalk.

"Business before pleasure," says Collins, with a twinkle in his eye. "I couldn't stop to say howdy-do till we were down here."

"You needn't stop to say it now," I says, mad all over.

"Now, Binney," says he, "no hard feelings. We couldn't have you mousing around up there—now, could we? If you were in my place wouldn't you do just what I did?"

I suppose I would, but that didn't have anything to do with it, that I could see.

"You might as well give it up," says Collins. "You've made a bully try, and you had us scared. Two boys couldn't have done better. You're all right."

We weren't looking for compliments, but, just the same, I couldn't help feeling Collins was a pretty good sort of a fellow. He was doing wrong, but he didn't realize it. I don't believe it's as bad to do wrong when you don't know you're doing wrong as it is to do wrong on purpose. But I may be mistaken.

"I'm going to stand half-way up the stairs," says Collins, "an' I'm not going to let you past. No good to try. I'll be as gentle as I can, but you'd better own up you're beaten. Don't feel bad about it. You put up a dandy fight."

Mark Tidd was pinching his cheek and squinting his eyes. Somehow that made me feel a little lighter inside. I'd been feeling like I'd swallowed a ton of lead by mistake.

"Well," says Mark, "we m-m-might as well git away from here."

"That's the spirit," says Collins. "But, all the same, I'll be standing right on those stairs, so don't try any monkey-shines."

"Come on, Binney," says Mark, as down-hearted as could be. We walked to the corner and turned. "Now r-r-run," says Mark. He started off helter-skelter, and I stuck right by him. At the back corner of the building he stopped. "Over the f-f-fence," he panted.

We were over in a jiffy, and then over the next fence, and that brought us into the back yard of the yellow-brick building.

I guess Mark had been expecting to go up the back stairs and get in that way, but the stairs were all built in and there was a padlock on the door. Mark stood looking at it like it had reached out and slapped him, then he looked up at the second story as if he thought maybe he'd try to jump.

"Um!" says he. "Um!" Then he began looking all around. At last he banged his right fist against his other hand and pointed to a low barn on the back of the lot that faced the next street. "Can we get up th-th-there?" he asked.

"If it'll do any good," says I.

"It may," says he.

We went back to the fence and climbed to the top of it. Right here came the first piece of luck we'd had for a long time: there was a painter's ladder in that yard lying against the barn.

In a minnit we had it up against the side and were scrambling to the roof. In two minnits we were perched on the ridge-pole, looking across at the window of the office where Uncle Hieronymous was shut in with Jiggins and the lawyer.

"What good is this?" I says.

"Attract his attention," says Mark.

"How?"

"Yell," says he.

I did. "Uncle Hieronymous!" I hollered, as loud as I could. "Uncle Hierony-mous!"

If the window across had been open it might have been all right, but, as it was, nothing happened at all. I tried again. It didn't do a bit of good.

"Well," says I, feeling like I could beller, "we're beat."

It did seem hard to come out at the little end of it when we were so close. It looked like it ought to be so easy to warn Uncle Hieronymous when he was only a hundred feet or so away. But it wasn't easy. It looked like it was impossible.

"Got to f-f-find some other way," says Mark.

"There isn't any," says I.

"Must be," says he. "*Got* to be. L-lemme think."

He thought and thought, and pinched his cheek and squinted his eyes, but it didn't seem like he was doing any good. After a while he sighed — a regular whop-per of a sigh.

"We hain't doin' any good here," he says. "Have to t-try somewheres else."

"Hain't got time," says I.

"Got half an hour, maybe. There'll be dickerin'. Your uncle won't make no deal till he's argued and fussed around c-consid'able. He's one of them kind. They hain't been there long, and Uncle Hieronymous never'll sell a farm in less'n an hour."

I wasn't so sure of that, and it didn't look like much to depend on, but Mark don't often go wrong when he's figgerin' out what folks'll do. He's the greatest fellow for knowing how anybody'll act that you ever saw.

"Come on," says he, beginning to scramble down off the shed.

"Where to?" I asked.

"Anywheres but here," says he. "It makes me mad to see them so close and not be able to d-d-do anything."

So down we slid into the yard again.

# CHAPTER XX

It looked pretty much to me like we were giving up—sort of deserting the ship. There we had been where we could actually *see* uncle and Jiggins and Collins, and we were going some place else. It seemed as if getting down off that roof and losing sight of them was about the same thing as running away. But then I looked at Mark. His chin stuck out like the cow-catcher on an engine. If I was going to draw a picture of Determination I'd have it look just like Mark did then. That was a little comfort.

"We got to hurry," says I, sort of nervous-like.

"Hurry where?" says Mark, with just the commencement of a grin.

Well, there I was. I hadn't any more idea what we ought to do than the man in the moon.

Mark started through the yard for the street. We climbed the first fence and that took us back of a hardware store—an area full of boxes and crates and all sorts of rubbish. We had to pick our way up close to the building. As we passed the door I saw Mark stop and stoop down. When he got up there was a coil of old half-inch rope in his hands—and he was grinning. I could see in a minnit he'd got his idea.

"Wait a s-s-second," says he, and he hurried into the store and up to a man standing by the counter.

"L-l-lemme take this r-rope," he stuttered, all out of breath. "I need it b-bad. Bring it back s-s-sure." You never heard such stuttering!

"Say that over ag'in, young feller," says the man.

"I want to b-b-borrow this rope," spluttered Mark, getting sort of mad.

The man grinned. "That there's a perty valuable rope," he said. "I dun'no's I got a more valuable piece'n that. I'm right down proud of that rope, I am. Don't no-ways calc'late to lose it. Got any security, young feller?"

In a second Mark had out his watch, snapped it off his chain, and laid it down on the counter.

"There," says he, and fairly ran out of the store with the rope in his hand. He went out the front door, and I after him.

"Now what?" I asked.

He didn't say a word, but just began coiling that rope as careful as if it was made of solid gold and he was afraid of scratching it. And all the time Uncle Hieronymous was in that room with those two men. By this time, maybe, they had his mine all taken away from him.

"Hurry!" says I. "Hurry! Hurry!"

"Don't do to h-hurry too much," says he. "Slow and careful. Take no chances."

By this time his rope was all coiled, and he began making a little loop in one end—a little loop about two inches long.

"What's that?" I asked, too anxious to keep still. It made me almost crazy to see him so deliberate.

He didn't answer, but just doubled the rope a ways from the noose and shoved it through the little loop. Then I saw. He was making a lasso.

It sort of disgusted me, for I couldn't see what good in the world a lasso could do, but he seemed satisfied. He made his noose just the right size to suit him and stretched it and put his foot in it to pull out all the crinkles.

"There," says he, just like he'd been trying to invent an airship and it had turned out to suit him. "Now," says he to me, "listen c-careful and don't make any mistakes."

"Go ahead," says I.

"We're going to the st-st-stairs where Collins is," says he. "When we g-get there you start to go up. Stamp with your feet and m-make a lot of noise. As soon as Collins sees you, begin to m-make fun of him. Get him mad! Get him awful mad!"

"Fine!" says I. "And let him catch me and give me a wallopin', too, I expect."

"No," says Mark. "Make him ch-ch-chase you."

"Great!" I says, sarcastic-like.

"Make him chase you," he repeated, "and be sure to turn this way. Remember, turn this way. Be sure he's so mad he'll chase you."

"Well," says I, "I don't see any sense to it, but maybe you know what you're up to with your chases and your lasso and one thing and another. Here goes!"

I started for the stairs, leaving Mark standing close to a telephone-pole with his lasso in his hand. When I turned in the doorway I saw Collins at the head of the stairs with his back turned. I stamped on the first step. Quick as a wink he turned around.

"Git out of there," says he.

"Peanuts," says I, aggravating-like, and took another step up.

"Binney," says Collins, "don't go making any monkey-shines. Go on away before I have to spank you."

"Huh!" I says. "Spank! A-a-aw!"

He began to look cross, and I went up two more steps, ready, you can bet, to turn and run just the minnit he looked like he was after me.

"Don't be sassy, Binney," Collins says. "It isn't becoming to small boys."

I went up another step. He started to come down, but not fast. I could see he wasn't real good and mad yet, so I didn't run. Then I had an idea myself. It isn't very often I get one, so I want credit for this. I remembered that I had a few bits of gravel in my pocket—round pebbles I'd figured on using some day in my slingshot. I reached for one and shot it at Collins just like you shoot a marble. It went whizz past his ear.

Now that would make anybody mad, wouldn't it—to have a kid shooting pebbles at him? He said something sharp. I shot another pebble, and it hit his hat. At that he let out a yell—a *mad* yell—and jumped for me.

Maybe you think I didn't get down those stairs quick. I don't remember touching my feet at all. Seems like I made it in one leap and lit running. Collins was right at my heels, and I could almost feel his hand on my collar. I was scairt, all right, but I didn't forget to turn the way Mark told me to. In a second I scudded past him where he stood by the telephone-pole holding his lasso. As I passed I saw him begin to twirl the noose.

Then I heard Collins say something that sounded like, "Wo-oo-of!" only louder and more surprised; and there was a scrape and a scuffle. I grabbed a hitching-post and stopped sudden. There was Collins in a heap on the sidewalk, with the lasso around his body and one arm, and Mark giving the rope a turn around his post and pulling like all-git-out.

"Q-quick!" he stuttered. "Up-stairs."

I understood then and dived for the stairway. Mark gave another jerk on the lasso, sprawling Collins over, and came after me. Up we went, making a clatter like a runaway team crossing a wooden bridge. We were pretty nearly at the top before Collins got loose and reached the bottom.

The way was clear before us to the door of the lawyer's office where Uncle Hieronymous was, but Collins was coming fast. He came up so fast his feet on the stairs sounded like he was playing a snare-drum. But he couldn't catch us. There was only thirty feet to go, and it was plain running. We ran!

And then! When we were not more than six feet from that door it opened and out stepped Jiggins!

Maybe he'd heard the racket, maybe he wanted a breath of air—I don't know what brought him, but there he was. He was no slow thinker, either. One glance showed him what was up, showed him Collins's head just coming into sight. His mouth set, and he plunged for Mark, who was at my side, made a grab at him with one hand and at me with the other.

He got Mark, but missed me. I stopped up and then dove at his legs just like I was playing football. He and Mark went down with a bang, and Collins, who was coming a mile a minute, went sprawling over them. In the scrimmage I got hold of one leg of Jiggins's and one of Collins's and held on. I couldn't see, because somebody rolled on top of me.

Next thing I knew I heard something rip, and saw Mark squirm and roll away toward the door. He was heavy and fat, but you should have seen how he got to his feet! Then he fairly dived at the door. It banged open, and he went down, rolling over and over on the floor right up to Uncle Hieronymous's feet.

HE WENT DOWN, ROLLING OVER AND OVER RIGHT UP TO UNCLE HIERONYMOUS'S FEET

Uncle Hieronymous yelled, "Woosh!" frightened-like, and jumped up on his feet.

Mark didn't wait to get up; he just laid there and hollered as loud as he could.

"Don't s-s-sell it! Don't have anything to d-do with 'em. They're—"

At that Collins, mad as the very dickens, got into the room and started to go for Mark. Uncle didn't know very clear what was going on, but he did know there was a man looking like he didn't mean anything friendly to a boy, so what does he do but step spry over Mark and take holt of Collins. I hadn't any idea uncle was so strong. Why, he put his hands under Collins's arms and just naturally lifted him up into the air.

"Stiddy! Stiddy, there!" he says, mild-like. "What's this here, eh? What's all this rollin' and plungin' and rampagin' around?" He sort of grinned friendly into Collins's face, still holdin' him in the air.

By that time Mark was up, and I got into the room, with Jiggins at my heels. I stole a look at Jiggins, and he sure did look queer—he looked beaten.

Mark looked at him too. "You're beat, Mr. Jiggins," says he. "You're b-b-beat."

Jiggins never said a word. Then Uncle Hieronymous put Collins down on his feet.

"Easy, now," he told him. "Stand without hitchin', mister." Then he turned to Mark and me. "What in tunket be you boys doin' here?" he asked, looking puzzled and sort of vague. "Didn't I leave you back to Baldwin, eh? Didn't I?"

"Have you signed anything?" asked Mark.

"Nary thing," says Uncle Hieronymous.

"Hurray!" says Mark, and I joined in.

"What's all this rumpus about?" uncle asked, wagging his head and tugging at his mustache.

Jiggins pushed past me and tried to speak, but uncle looked at him queer-like, and says:

"Mister, I guess you better let this here boy talk a spell. Seems like I'm hankerin' to hear him worse'n I be you."

"But—" says Jiggins.

"I don't want to speak to you noways but kind," says uncle, beginning to frown a little, "but it runs in my head you been up to somethin', mister. Now you jest keep still till Marcus Tidd gits in his say."

Jiggins remembered how uncle had hoisted Collins, and didn't say another word. As for the lawyer-man, he was edging toward the door.

"Well?" says Uncle Hieronymous.

Then we told him, each of us trying to talk at once. We told him everything from the beginning. We described how we got suspicious of Collins, and how we found the letter and the telegram, and what we overheard on the lake, and how we escaped from the cabin, and all about our race down the river.

Uncle kept saying "Oh!" and "Ah!" and "Goodness gracious!" and grunting like he was astonished most out of his head.

"A mine!" says he, when we were through. "Copper! Um! Who'd 'a' thought it? Not me. Nor Alfred. Hain't that fine, now? I'm happy, eh? Alfred's happy. Marthy and Mary'll be happy." For a minnit he didn't say a word; then he turned to Collins and Jiggins, and you wouldn't believe how dignified he looked in that minnit. "And," says he, gentle-like, but accusingly, "you tried to git it away from me for three hundred dollars. I hadn't never done you no despite, had I? No. Then why did you fellers try to do this? Don't seem noways decent nor Christian to act like you done. I guess," he says, sorry-like, "that I don't want to talk to you no more. Come on, boys. Let's go away from here."

We went out of the door and left Jiggins & Co. standing there. I looked back. They looked *ashamed*. Yes, sir; ashamed is the word. They weren't looking at each other at all, but at the floor. Somehow I felt ashamed for them. I didn't say a word to them, nor did Mark.

When we got out into the street uncle stopped and grabbed his leg between his thumb and finger and pinched it good.

"'Tain't no nightmare, is it?" he asked. "Them men was there, and there is a mine, eh? No mistake?"

"There's a mine," says Mark, "and it's worth a l-l-lot of money."

"To be sure," says Uncle Hieronymous. "Mines generally is. Well, well! Who'd 'a' thought it? Copper under that ol' forty. Marcy me! What had I best do? I dun'no' what to do about it."

"See a good lawyer," says Mark. "He'll know."

"Dun'no' any lawyer," says Uncle Hieronymous.

Mark slapped his leg. "I know one," says he, "and he's one you can t-t-trust, too. Name's Macmillan. We met him fishin' b-b-back of your house."

I remembered him right off and knew in a second he'd be a good man to go to.

"Come on," says Mark. "Let's find him."

So off we went looking for Mr. Macmillan. Uncle made up another poem as we went along:

> "I never seen sich a surprise;
> It most knocks out a feller's eyes."

I expect it did pretty nearly surprise him to death.

# CHAPTER XXI

It was easy to find Mr. Macmillan. Everybody seemed to know him. His office was up over the bank. When we got there he was in, but at first he didn't recognize us.

"D-don't you remember the boys you m-met while you was f-f-fishin' a week ago?"

"Of course," says he. "Of course I do. Sit right down and tell me what I can do for you."

"This is Mister Hieronymous Alphabet Bell," says Mark. "He's B-Binney Jenks's uncle."

"Glad to know you, Mr. Bell," says Mr. Macmillan. "I hope you're well."

Uncle answered him in poetry:

> "I got my health; I got my breath,
> But I'm clost to bein' s'prised to death."

Mr. Macmillan's face twitched like he wanted to laugh, but he didn't. He was as polite as could be.

"What's the cause of the surprise, Mr. Bell?"

"You tell him," says uncle to Mark. "I hain't got so's I can speak yet."

Mark told all about it, while Mr. Macmillan's eyes got bigger and bigger and more and more astonished.

"You don't mean to tell me you boys worked all this out just from seeing a letter, and that you outwitted those two men? It doesn't come within the bounds of possibility."

"Everything I s-said," says Mark, sort of dignified, "we did."

"I beg your pardon," says Mr. Macmillan. "I didn't doubt your word, of course. But it's so remarkable. You are remarkable boys."

I shook my head. "Mark's a remarkable boy," says I. "All I did was come along."

Mr. Macmillan shook his head. "You both deserve a lot of credit. As for me, I'm proud I know you. Now let's get down to business. What are you going to do about it all?"

"We d-d-don't know," says Mark. "That's why we came to you."

Mr. Macmillan turned and looked at his desk. For fifteen minutes he thought it over, and then he says, "I guess we better have a talk with Jiggins & Co. Can you find them?"

"I guess so," I says. "I'll go and see."

I hustled right over to the hotel, and there, in the office, sat Jiggins and Collins, looking pretty glum, I can tell you. I went straight up to them.

"Mr. Macmillan wants to know if you'll please come up to his office," says I.

Jiggins began to sing his funny little tune. "Tum-a-diddle, dum-a-diddle, dum-a-diddle-dee," and so on. Then he smiled sort of sickly.

"Well, Binney," says he, "you beat, after all, didn't you?"

"Mark Tidd comes pretty close to beatin' every time," I says.

"Yes," says Jiggins, "I expect he does. Looks like he would. Wonderful boy. Knew he was wonderful all the time. Liked him. Still like him. Always will like him. No hard feelings. Not a one. Don't hold a thing up against him."

"That's good," says I, "because Mark and I don't hold no grudge against you and Mr. Collins. You wasn't doin' right, but maybe that wasn't your fault. Maybe you wasn't taught jest proper. You're the pleasantest villains I ever knew."

At that both Collins and Jiggins laughed. "First time I ever thought of myself as a villain," says Collins.

"Who's Mr. Macmillan?" says Jiggins.

"He's our lawyer."

"Oh," says Jiggins, and he laughed again, but this time it was a pale sort of laugh. "You don't let grass grow under your feet."

"Not when we're fussin' with you, Mr. Jiggins," says I, meaning a compliment.

He took it that way, and smiled like he was pleased.

"Will you come?" I asked him.

"To be sure. Why not? Nothing else to do. Got to bargain now. Cost more money. Ugh! Hate to think how much."

We went right up to Mr. Macmillan's office, and I introduced Collins and Jiggins to him.

"Who are you acting for?" asked Mr. Macmillan.

"The United States Copper Company," says Jiggins.

"Have you authority to make an agreement on this matter?"

"Yes," says Jiggins.

"Well," says Mr. Macmillan, "I've thought this over, and I guess a royalty on tonnage will be the best plan for Mr. Bell."

"What's a royalty on t-t-tonnage?" asked Mark.

"It means that the company will pay Mr. Bell a certain amount for every ton of copper it takes out of his mine."

Mark nodded his head.

"That would be most satisfactory to us," says Jiggins.

Then they went to arguing and dickering and talking and talking for hours, it seemed. Then Mr. Macmillan called in his stenographer and dictated an agreement to her. The agreement read that the company was to pay to Uncle Hieronymous or his heirs three thousand dollars every year for fifty years. They were to pay that much at the very least. That was what Mr. Macmillan called a minimum. Mark saved up that word. But uncle might get more. If the company took out so much copper that the royalties came to more than three thousand dollars a year, uncle would get whatever it was. He might get nothing but the three thousand dollars every year, and then, again, he might get ten or twenty times as much.

Uncle Hieronymous sat like he was dreaming. Every once in a while he'd break out with some sort of an exclamation like "Shucks!" or "Ginger!" or "I swanny!"

The agreement was written after a while.

"You send this to be signed by the proper officers of your company," says Mr. Macmillan. "When it comes back with the three thousand dollars for the first year Mr. Bell will sign, too. Then the matter will be settled."

Well, Jiggins sent the contract to his company, and they signed it and sent back the money. That fixed it so Uncle Hieronymous was rich. Think of it! Three thousand dollars every year, and maybe more! He couldn't get used to it, and kept saying he didn't know what to do with it and it would be a burden to him. Mark told him he'd find ways to use it and he needn't worry.

How proud he was of Mark and me! He never stopped talking about us and what we did and making poems about it. One of the poems I remember. It said:

> "Oh, Binney Jenks and Marcus Tidd,
> It beats the dickens what you did!"

Now, isn't that a dandy compliment?

Well, when everything was settled we said good-by to Mr. Macmillan and to Collins and Jiggins. They had got over their disappointment and were quite pleasant again. They came down to the depot to see us off, and Jiggins gave both of us a jack-knife. They were dandies, too, with a corkscrew, a hammer, a saw, a glass-cutter, a file, and lots of other tools in them.

We shook hands all around, and somehow I was sorry to see the last of them. They were the pleasantest enemies in the world. Then the train started off, and we were on our way to Baldwin again.

My! but Tallow and Plunk were glad to see us, and Martha and Mary were so tickled to see Uncle Hieronymous they almost scared him to death. He hired a man to go and drive Alfred back from the farm where he'd left him.

We boys stayed with him a whole month, and I want to tell you we had the best time ever. It was a lot better than it would have been, because all the while we were so glad we had helped to make Uncle Hieronymous rich.

At last we had to start for home, and uncle drove us to the train behind Alfred. He was most crying when he said good-by, but he promised to come and see us a long time next winter. The last thing he said was a poem.

"I do admire Marcus Tidd.
He surely is the smartest kid."

And Tallow and Plunk and I agreed with him. Don't you think so, too?

**THE END**

Lector House believes that a society develops through a two-fold approach of continuous learning and adaptation, which is derived from the study of classic literary works spread across the historic timeline of literature records. Therefore, we aim at reviving, repairing and redeveloping all those inaccessible or damaged but historically as well as culturally important literature across subjects so that the future generations may have an opportunity to study and learn from past works to embark upon a journey of creating a better future.

This book is a result of an effort made by Lector House towards making a contribution to the preservation and repair of original ancient works which might hold historical significance to the approach of continuous learning across subjects.

HAPPY READING & LEARNING!

**LECTOR HOUSE LLP**
**E-MAIL:** lectorpublishing@gmail.com

www.ingramcontent.com/pod-product-compliance
Lightning Source LLC
Chambersburg PA
CBHW051217160726
47994CB00002B/633